Christmas in HEAVEN

Christmas in HEAVEN

Carol Lynch Williams

G. P. Putnam's Sons • New York

To my father, who has given me all that I have,
including my bit of Heaven—my family

G. P. PUTNAM'S SONS
a division of Penguin Putnam Books for Young Readers, 345 Hudson Street, New
York, NY 10014. G. P. Putnam's Sons, Reg. U.S. Pat. & Tm. Off.
Published simultaneously in Canada. Printed in the United States of America.
Designed by Semadar Megged
Text set in 12-point Horley Old Style
Library of Congress Cataloging-in-Publication Data

Williams, Carol Lynch.
Christmas in Heaven / Carol Lynch Williams.
p. cm.
Summary: When a self-centered famous movie star builds a mansion near her
family's diner in an isolated part of Florida, twelve-year-old Honey develops
a friendship with the younger daughter that helps Honey realize
how special her own family is.
[1. Family life—Florida—Fiction. 2. Friendship—Fiction. 3. Parent and
child—Fiction. 4. Christian life—Fiction. 5. Florida—Fiction.] I. Title.
PZ7.W65588 Ch 2000
[Fic] 21—dc21
99-043155

ISBN 0-399-23436-5
3 5 7 9 10 8 6 4 2

Chapter 1

I LIVE IN HEAVEN.

No, I'm not dead and buried, though I know it's gonna happen someday. And I have to admit I'm not looking forward to it one little bit.

I live in Heaven, Florida. It's a tiny place a billion miles from anywhere. It's so small that we're not a town really. We don't even have an official name, just one that Momma made up.

When we'd been here a couple of years she went out and painted a great big sign. It said: You're Entering and Leaving Heaven—Right This Very Second (pop 6). The sign is still up, right across from our diner, though I will admit the blue of the paint has faded some. For a while we had a "pop" of ten. But things change, just like you'll see in this story.

Used to be only three families lived here.

'Course there's us. We're the DeLoaches.

"What are we doin' here?" my brother always says. His name is Bill, after Daddy's daddy, William Harold. I call him Willie-Bill 'cause it nearly drives him crazy. I like to watch his face turn red.

But getting back to that question of Willie-Bill's, "What are we doin' here?" He says it leaning up against the huge oak that holds our two-story tree house. Or leaning on the counter of the diner, when he should be cleaning up. Or when he's bored. Or when we're tending our little vegetable stand. Or when it's too hot. Or when it's too cold. Or when there's a full moon. Or when there isn't.

Momma says he asks this question 'cause he's fourteen.

I say, "Hell, Momma. Just how many times before he's memorized the answer?"

Momma laughs and says, "Honey." That's my real name. "When you're fourteen you'll be asking the same thing."

Yeah, right. I don't think so.

I guess I should tell you Momma lets me say two curse words: hell and damn.

You'd like my momma. Her full name is Sarah Amanda McKenna DeLoach, but she goes by Mandy. She's always wearing summery tops with long skirts that almost reach her ankles. She has really wild hair that goes just past her shoulder blades. It's curly and the color of rich soil. She exercises all the time and pushes health food on truck drivers. And even if they hate alfalfa sprouts and raw mushrooms on their turkey burgers, they buy it because they like Momma, too.

The reason I can say hell and damn is Pop-Pop. He's my momma's daddy and he's a born-again preacher. He lives in Orlando. You've probably seen him on TV. He's on *Five Alive* every morning at 5 A.M. He makes good money telling people about hellfire and brimstone. Pop-Pop's the one who's convinced me that I don't wanna die. And he believes a soul's gotta get saved. Getting saved is one of those things I set up close to dying: I'm not looking forward to it either, though I have to admit I've tried. To get saved, I mean.

But let me get back to telling about the people here in Heaven.

My daddy, Joseph Samuel DeLoach, cooks for the Straight from Heaven diner. It's our very own place. He used to be a defense lawyer. But he got sick of living where there was so much crime and where there were so many people. So he moved us all from Miami to Heaven. That was when I was seven and Willie-Bill was nine. And I do believe that Willie-Bill has been complaining ever since.

Daddy bought a hundred acres of grassland with the intention of us raising cattle. In the middle of building our house, though, he changed his mind. No cows for him, he said. He wanted to be a cook. So he had a diner built next to the highway, close to the only gas station for miles and miles.

Now you'd think, us being so far from anything, there'd be no business for a diner, but that just isn't the case. We're set right off a major two-lane highway that leads everybody from central Florida directly to the beach. On weekends we get more than enough business to keep us going all the winter long. That and the fact that Daddy does lots of writing for lawyer-type people. But that's way too boring to dig around in.

Lyman Hiatt and his son, Taylor, are the official workers at the Sinclair green-dinosaur gas station. You know, the gas station that's mascot is an apatosaurus. Pretty much, not including the weekday truck drivers, their business is our business, and I mean that in more ways than one.

Taylor is one week older than Willie-Bill. His momma left him and his daddy just two years after Taylor entered the world.

"Not that I blame her," Willie-Bill said once to Momma. She near about tore his head off.

"Don't you ever say anything like that again, Mr. DeLoach."

"Uh," was the only thing he had the chance to answer.

"No mother should ever leave her child."

"This flyspeck on a map done her in," Willie-Bill whispered to me later. "His momma left 'cause she was bored outta her head."

Taylor's always saying to me, "Honey, that red hair of yours sets my heart afire."

Red hair nothing. It's auburn.

"And those puppy-dog eyes of yours make my stomach flip-flop."

Sure, my eyes are brown, but they aren't a thing dog-like.

I can't complain to Momma about that 'cause she's always telling me I'm pretty. But what does being pretty matter when the only boy around is Taylor Hiatt?

"Honey," Taylor says. "I'm gonna be a writer. I may not make much money, but I'll never starve. And I want to marry you."

Just between the two of us, there are some days when Taylor talks to me and my face colors with pleasure. 'Course, other days I want to run screaming into the road. But that wouldn't do me a lick a good unless it was the weekend.

So I ignore both Taylor and Willie-Bill.

That used to be all the people there were living here.

Then one Tuesday I was riding my bike out on the two-lane highway. And I noticed that someone was building a house. A great big ol' thing.

Almost a year later Christmas came to Heaven and things haven't been the same since.

Chapter 2

ONE SUNNY THURSDAY MORNING, ME, MOMMA, and Daddy watched three big American Van Line trucks zoom past the diner headed in the direction of "The Mansion." That's what we called the house as soon as the frame was up, 'cause it was so big and all.

The whole family was preparing for when we opened at noon. I polished silverware. Daddy and Momma did food prep. You know, chopping, slicing, and dicing fruits and vegetables for later. Willie-Bill was supposed to be folding the red-and-yellow checked napkins into small teepees. Mostly, though, he just sat and did nothing but complain that all he ever did was slave around this place. Okay, so the whole family *wasn't* working.

Taylor was visiting. The faint smell of gasoline sat in a small cloud around him. It follows him everywhere. Kind of like that cloud of dust that hovers over Pigpen in those old Charlie Brown cartoons. Now Taylor watched me from a shiny red leather booth that he had wiped down. One of Willie-Bill's chores.

Whenever I looked up, I caught him staring.

"What?" I finally said, then I pretended to throw a knife at him. He pretended I hit him in the chest.

"Right in the heart, Honey," he said. "In my heart full of love for you."

"Puh-lease," I said, and started polishing all the faster. I had to get out of the diner and away from my brother and his friend. They were both driving me nuts.

And, anyway, there were three American Van Lines to be unloaded. An inspector of goods was needed. I nominated myself to the job.

"Momma, I'm done," I said after catching Taylor staring at me about the one hundredth time. "I'm going to see if The Mansion's gonna have any kids living in it. I'm telling you, we need some new blood around here." I looked straight at Willie-Bill and Taylor when I said that.

Willie-Bill started to fold his fourth napkin.

Taylor blew me a kiss.

I threatened him with a fork that I picked up off a table when I passed, dropping it on the pile of cloth that Willie-Bill sat moaning and complaining near.

"See you later, baby," Daddy said.

Then I pushed outside.

"Be back in time for the lunch crowd," Momma said.

"Yes, ma'am," I said.

The door jangled closed. Summer air, smelling a little like cooked grass, swept over me. I started sweating right away. In the distance the sky piled high with thunderclouds. At around three o'clock this afternoon the rains would come and cool things off. It happened that way every day. Always before dinner, nearly always the same time, like maybe the weather kept a watch tucked somewhere so it'd be punctual.

Our house sits back behind the diner a good half mile. We never take the family car down here, 'cause we're so close. That's another thing Willie-Bill complains about. We all bike down and park our bicycles in different places behind the diner when we're at work. Mine's always next to the gas meter.

I got on my purple bike and started pedaling like crazy. It wasn't but a few minutes till I had gone the two miles to where the vans had already backed into the driveway.

I knew I wouldn't be able to see too good if I stayed down near the mailbox so I pedaled up to an orange truck.

There were four men grunting in and out of the van, struggling down the metal ramp with boxes and furniture.

All of them pretended to ignore me. I pretended like I didn't give a care, and really I didn't. I just wanted to find out who had built this big house and I thought they might be able to tell me.

When one of them, a balding guy whose pants were riding low on his backside, accidentally glanced in my direction I started up a conversation.

"Sure is hot," I said.

He didn't answer but oozed out a breath of air. He carried one side of a big-screen television that had an orange blanket draped over it. The blanket said American Van Lines.

"That must be heavy," I said.

The balding man didn't say anything. Somehow he had gotten stuck with the walking backward part and he was feeling around with his foot for the steps.

"Don't trip," I said, hoping that he might. Not that I wanted him to get hurt or anything. I didn't, for sure. But I did think it might be kind of funny to watch him and the pointy-beard guy on the other side struggle to keep such an expensive TV from getting broken.

I followed the men back and forth from the truck to the front doors of the house over and over again. Finally the balding guy said, "Kid, just what is it you want?"

I felt a little indignant about the kid part but decided to take what Daddy would call a window of opportunity.

"I'm just wondering if any people my age come with all this stuff?" I emphasized the words "people my age," then gestured at the inside of the huge truck. I shaded my eyes, then tried to give the man the puppy-dog look Taylor says I have. It didn't soften this guy's heart none. He just mopped at his forehead with his hand then threw the sweat on the brick driveway.

"Yes," he said. "There are two kids that'll live here." He emphasized the word "kids."

I ignored it. No need to start a battle. This guy had the information I wanted.

"How old are they? And are they boys or girls?" I kept my fingers crossed for at least one girl. Boys were beginning to make me sick.

"I saw only one of 'em. And she was a girl . . . I think.

9

That's all I know. But I'm sure she looked to be your age."

"Well, what *did* she look like?" I asked. I had to lean into the back of the truck because he'd walked in to get more stuff. The truck was warm where I touched it with my hands, and my shoulders and head came just above the floor, what with it being so high off the ground and all. I noticed the strong smell of metal and sweat.

"Honey," he said, turning around. He had a look of real irritation on his face.

"Why, how'd you know my name?" I asked, like I was surprised, but I wasn't. I play that trick on everybody.

"What?" the man said with a grunt.

"I said Honey really is my name."

He staggered out with a box and carried it into the house. After a few seconds he was back. He came up close to me and said, "Whoever you are, we got this truck—" he pointed to the one that they'd all been working in. "—those trucks—" he pointed to the ones that sat open. "—and one more to unload that isn't even here yet."

I gave a low whistle to show him I was impressed.

"I cannot answer your questions about what or who or when or why."

"I'll stand around here and watch yawl take things out," I said. "I can get plenty of clues from watching, you know." And then to be polite I added, "If that's okay with you." I smiled as pretty as I could.

"Watch all you want, just don't ask no questions—"

"And you'll tell me no lies," I interrupted.

The man stared at me.

"Can you please tell me what your names are?" I had been thinking about them each in a different way. Baldy. He was the one I was talking to. Pointy Chin—the guy with the beard. Young-Kid. He was the one who looked to be only a little older than Willie-Bill. And The Spitter. He was the guy who could spit half a mile sure.

"I'm Bob. That's Ted. That's Carol and that's Alice." Bob pointed out everyone as he spoke. A couple of the guys chuckled. But I didn't argue. How could I with a name like Honey?

Chapter 3

A WEEK LATER NO ONE STILL HAD MOVED INTO The Mansion. I know 'cause I was keeping an eye on things.

It was Friday afternoon and traffic was getting thick. Daddy was back at the grill, making sure that we had everything we'd need for the weekend. People would be stopping in any minute now.

Momma wiped down all the tabletops and the countertops, too.

Willie-Bill was supposed to be laying out place settings, but he was complaining about the heat outside, even though it was nice and cool in the diner.

I dusted all the large black-and-white pictures of famous old movie stars we have hanging on the walls. There was Audrey Hepburn and James Dean and John Wayne and Fred Astaire and a dozen more. And a big picture of Pop-Pop, too. He was the only alive movie star on the wall. Only he's not really a movie star.

When I got done I went over and helped put out the place settings.

The bell rang saying someone had come in for dinner and I looked up. There stood three people in the doorway. And they were definitely not going to the beach.

The woman, the mother, I guessed, was dressed in a pair of tight white pants and a shiny blue sleeveless top. Her blond hair was frozen in a huge puffy design, with glittering things stuck everywhere in it.

The older girl was in leather. She had a nose ring and her hair was the same color as her fingernails. Black. Everything was color coordinated to match her hair and nails. Except for a pair of red leather boots.

Then there was the last girl. I knew at once that this was who Baldy Bob had been talking about. And I could see why he hadn't known if she was a girl or not. Her blond hair was real short and cut jagged like she'd done the job herself. She didn't have any rings at all. Not in her ears or on her hands or in her nose. She wore a pair of blue jeans and a loose shirt that was way too big for her. In fact, she reminded me of me. Except she was embarrassed.

In all my life I've never been embarrassed by my family. Not even Willie-Bill. He just bugs me half to death. But this girl was embarrassed.

The lady in the shiny top spread her arms out wide and said in a loud voice, "Where shall we sit, children? I hope the lack of customers here is not indicative of the food or service." There was something vaguely familiar about this woman.

I wasn't sure what "indicative" meant, but I could tell

by Momma's face that *she* knew and that she was not happy.

"Sit anywhere you'd like," Momma said, forcing herself to be customer oriented. Sometimes that can be a chore.

"How quaint," the woman said. She and her leather daughter sat in a corner booth. The younger girl came up to the counter and sat down near to where I stood.

"Christmas, come over here," the lady said.

"No, thank you," Christmas said. She didn't look back, just at her hands. I noticed her nails were bitten down to the nubs.

Christmas, I thought. That was an even more weird name than Honey. Or those two guys being named Carol and Alice, for that matter.

"Easter and I will miss you." The voice sang across the diner.

Easter? I felt my head jerk to look at the girl in black. I couldn't even control my neck I was so surprised by the name. Easter?

"We recently moved into the neighborhood," the woman continued.

Daddy had poked his head out the opening in the wall between the grill and the diner. I noticed his hair, pulled back in a short ponytail, was starting to come undone because of how hard he was working.

"Is that so," said Momma.

Willie-Bill moved lickety-split to fill all the glasses

with water. It was a miracle to see him go so fast. He nod-ded his head at Easter.

The door chimed again and a group of kids came inside.

"Honey," Momma said, and I started hustling, hand-ing out menus and replacing silverware.

We were busy from then on, until we closed the diner at 11 P.M. I never did have a chance to talk to Christmas because I was running back and forth all over the place getting orders, handing out menus, and making sure everyone had enough water in their red glass tumblers.

Before they had left, Christmas's mother had stood and in a too-loud voice thanked Momma for the splendid meal.

"For a place so shabby, I have been quite pleasantly surprised," she said.

Momma stood tight-lipped and didn't answer.

Then, from a booth near the door, a girl in a bikini with a Tweety Bird towel wrapped around her hips squealed, "It's Miriam Season."

The diner went quiet, except for Daddy, who said, "Order up, Mandy," to Momma. I could hear the fluo-rescent lights buzzing.

"Of course," I said. *That's* why she had looked so fa-miliar.

Every head turned and looked at Miriam Season. She pressed her hand on her large bosoms and smiled, show-ing all her big, white teeth. The diamond on her pointer finger and the gold and diamond tennis bracelet caught the fluorescent lights of the diner and glittered. Miriam Season twirled once in her high heel white shoes.

"Why," she said, "I didn't think I'd even be noticed, much less recognized, out here in the middle of nowhere." I heard Daddy start to laugh and then cough. Christmas put her head in her hands. A slow blush crept down her neck.

People jumped up from their seats.

"I saw you in *The Winds of Willoughby*. You were perfect."

"Your performances are flawless."

"Can I have your autograph?"

Christmas walked out the door.

Easter went back to the booth. She stretched her long legs onto the seat. When she didn't think anyone was looking, she gulped down the rest of her mother's beer in one breath. Then she saw me staring at her, and smiled. I tried to smile back, but I couldn't. The black lipstick was beginning to wear off Easter's lips, making it look like blood was seeping through.

Chapter 4

I DON'T KNOW HOW I KNEW THE SEASONS WERE the owners of The Mansion, but I did. Just like that. Somehow the three of them seemed to fit all together in glitter, leather, and embarrassment.

So on the following Monday morning, right after breakfast and family Bible reading time, I told Momma and Daddy I was headed off for an adventure.

"Where you planning on going?" Momma asked, raising her left eyebrow up the way Spock always does in the old *Star Trek* TV shows. Of course, I'm not sure which eyebrow Spock uses, but Momma does raise her left one.

"I'm headed down to The Mansion," I said. "I'm planning on visiting Christmas."

Willie-Bill appeared out of nowhere.

"Did she tell you that they live in that big ol' place?" he said.

"No, she did not," I said. "I figured it out on my own. Is it okay if I go, Momma?"

Daddy listened from his easy chair. He always tries to

relax after a big weekend. He likes this job, working only Thursday afternoon through Sunday night even though hours are long. And it's nice having him home. Before, when he was a lawyer, I didn't ever see him.

"I don't know," Momma said real slow. And I knew she was remembering Miriam Season saying not-so-nice things about the diner.

"I think you should let her go," said Willie-Bill.

I looked at him bug-eyed and slack jawed.

"I'll go along to make sure Honey doesn't get in trouble. There's always trouble at rich people's houses."

"What interest do you have over there, Bill?" Daddy said, like he already knew.

Willie-Bill's face got all red. It made the three pimples on his chin look an angry color.

"I don't need no help," I said to him.

"I don't need *any* help," Momma said, correcting me.

"Me neither," I said. "I been down to that place tons of times without you making sure I was safe, Willie-Bill. I don't need a baby-sitter now."

Willie-Bill walked over to where I stood and put his arm around me. I could smell his pits. It wasn't at all pleasant.

"Honey," he said. "Don't you ever look at *The Star* or *The Globe*? Those two papers are always reporting the facts about movie stars' places just the way they happen."

"Get away from me, you old foul-smelling demon," I said, jerking free of Willie-Bill's heavy arm. "Come out, foul demon" is something Pop-Pop is always saying Jesus would say to rid another of evil spirits. If anybody needed a cleansing right now, it was Willie-Bill.

"I think it would be all right for you to go visiting," Momma said. "It looked like that little girl needed a friend."

"Thanks, Momma," I said. I kissed her cheek.

"I think her sister needs a friend as well," said Willie-Bill. He kissed Momma, too. Then he followed me to the door.

"No way," I said. "You are not coming."

"I am so. This is a free country, don't you know."

"Yes, I do know. But you're still not coming. I'm the one who's been keeping tabs on this place. And I happen to be a girl like the rest of those people."

"So?"

"So," I said. I was starting to feel kind of mad. "So I'm going alone. Right, Daddy?"

I looked over at Daddy, who closed his eyes and rested in the sunlight like he didn't know what was going on.

"Right, Momma?"

"I think it's okay for you to go alone this time," she said.

"Oh, thanks, Momma," I said. "You're a true saint." That's something Pop-Pop calls people once they've accepted Jesus into their hearts. For a moment I knew what Pop-Pop meant. I felt real glad that Willie-Bill would be staying home today.

"I wouldn't want to be going anywhere anyway if I were you," I said as I hurried out to my bicycle. "Not if I had a carbuncle the size of the one you have on your chin."

I didn't hear Willie-Bill's answer. The screen door slammed behind me. I was off.

It was hot out, but not too humid. As I ran through the grass to the garage, grasshoppers flew left and right, humming their flight songs. I went past a red ant bed that was as big as a tire and as high as my knees. Daddy has been saying forever that he'd get rid of it, but it's kind of turned into an experiment. Just how big and dangerous will it get?

I got my bike and with a whir pushed off down our long driveway.

I took my time getting to The Mansion. *We'd* already had a huge breakfast. *We'd* already had our family time, when Daddy played the piano and Momma led us in a few church hymns. *We'd* already spent a few minutes doing our chores.

But what about famous people? Maybe they ate at a different time. Maybe they slept in real late. Maybe they didn't pray or clean.

So I went slow, enjoying the baked earth smell and the sun beating down on me. I rolled my bike along the road, zigzagging on the empty highway, breathing deep all the good smells and thoughts and feelings of my life right at that moment.

Up ahead, The Mansion rose tall. I was surprised at the bigness of it. Somehow I had missed just how large it is, what with my being so intent on seeing if there'd be kids living here. It was four or five times bigger than our place, and we have a good-sized home. I could see its six fireplaces. White, three-story columns lined the front porch. And in the back there was another house. Nowhere near as big, but made from the same red brick, with white columns and a porch. There was a pool, too. I couldn't see it, but the sun was stabbing at the water and reflected light slashed onto the screened-in area in the backyard. There was a tennis court and a six-car garage. The whole thing nearly took my breath away.

I parked my bike near the pink azalea bushes, then stood in front of the double doors that were full of glass. A large chandelier hung in the entry. That entry was near as big as our formal living room. I caught my reflection right when I rang the bell. My hair was windblown from the ride over. Using my fingers as a brush, I tried to straighten out the tangles, but it didn't really work.

A loud gong sound echoed through the house.

That's when I saw Willie-Bill. Sneaking up behind me, a little distorted in the glass.

I whirled around.

"Get outta here, you smelly creep," I said. "Momma said I could come alone. She's gonna be madder than a hornet."

Willie-Bill whistled low and came to stand up next to me, ignoring every damn word I had said.

"Look at this place," he said. "They got a swimming pool and everything here, Honey."

I noticed he had pinched his three pimples. The skin

was all red around them. There was a tiny bit of dried blood on his chin.

"I said get on home. Momma told you to let me come alone. Why'd you follow me here?"

A hot breeze blew across the stone front porch. It was right then the front door opened, almost without a sound. I might not have even known except for the cold air that rushed from the house and hit me in the back.

I turned to face the door.

A woman stood in front of us. She was dressed in a maid's uniform and seemed older than the hills. She had more wrinkles than should be allowed. She had my share and her own and someone else's to boot.

"What are you selling," the woman asked, only it wasn't a question.

"Nothing." She made me a little nervous. "I was wondering if Christmas could play today."

"Play?" the lady said. "She's a bit old for play. But she might be interested in a guest." The woman turned and walked away.

I stood still on the porch.

The lady turned then and said, "Well, come with me." She sounded bothered so I followed her, quick, into the house and shut the front door, quicker, right in Willie-Bill's face.

"Isn't the boy coming, too?" the lady asked. There was almost a hint of a question in her voice.

"No," I said. "He just followed me over to make sure I'd get here safe and sound."

Chapter 5

THE LADY WENT TO THE BOTTOM OF THE stairs. And let me tell you, these stairs were huge. And triple high. They curved around and landed here in the foyer. In the exact middle of the ceiling was the chandelier.

"Christmas," the old lady called, then she glanced back at me with a funny look on her face.

For some reason I felt like maybe I was supposed to make an excuse for her hollering.

"That's how we get people's attention at our house, too," I said. "We yell. At the top of our lungs, sometimes."

"I'm not at all surprised," the woman said, then she walked away and left me standing in the foyer.

I felt uneasy. I almost wished Willie-Bill *had* come inside. I looked back at the glass door. He had his face pressed to the pane. His nose was flat, his lips spread out thin.

Thank goodness, I thought, I *didn't* let him come in.

I heard a noise from upstairs and looked high above

me. There stood Easter. She still wore all black, only she had changed her boots. They were bright yellow. I didn't even know there were such things as bright yellow boots. But believe you me, there are at least one pair in this whole wide world.

Easter acted as though she didn't even see me. She disappeared back into somewhere above, then after a moment came out again. She threw something over the side of the banister and I leaped away. It was a ladder made of metal and rope. The last rung slapped against the tile floor, which was a cool pink color, making a ping sound. I watched Easter, openmouthed, as she slung her leg over the railing and began climbing down the swinging ladder. I noticed she had done something funny with her hair. One side was way shorter than the other. It hadn't looked like that the night they stopped in at the diner.

When Easter was about six feet from the floor, she jumped, landing in a crouch close enough to me that I felt the air move as she fell past.

"Can you tell me where I can get a good tattoo?" she asked from her squatting position.

I looked around to see if I was still alone in the foyer. I was. The only person even close was Willie-Bill. Now, not only was his nose pressed flat and broad, he was looking a bit bug-eyed. I hoped real hard he didn't leave a greasy print on the glass.

"Well, no, not really," I said. "I don't know much about tattoos."

"Your father doesn't have one?" Easter said.

I shook my head.

"Rumor has it that my father is covered with tattoos. His whole body. Rabbits. Hence my name."

All I could do was look at her. What do you say to someone when they tell you their father was a rabbit-tattooed man?

The rope ladder swung back and forth making a soft sound on the floor.

Easter stood, stretching herself out tall and dark. She seemed especially pale skinned. I wasn't sure if she was sick or if maybe her clothes made her look so white.

"You guys don't have anything in this funny place called Heaven."

It wasn't a question or a statement. It was more like an accusation and all of a sudden I felt responsible for not knowing where a good tattoo shop was.

"I want a black heart right here," Easter said, and she pointed to her throat, right where any vampire might want to take a bite. If he was brave enough, I mean.

"Christmas?" I said. It was the only word I could manage. The thought of a permanent black heart on Easter's throat made it hard to think of anything but that.

Easter threw her head back and shrieked for her sister. "Christmas, get the hell down here!" As God is my witness, I swear the windows rattled. Then she groped around in her shirt pocket and brought out a package of cigarettes.

I looked back at Willie-Bill. He gestured, making motions for me to open the door for him and I looked away quick, hoping he wouldn't all of a sudden get the sense of a gnat and ring the bell.

There was a loud noise from upstairs and Christmas came out to the banister. Her bare toes sunk into the thick pale pink carpet.

"What?" she said.

The doorbell donged then.

Easter jerked her thumb at me. "You have company, sister dear." Her voice was sarcastic. She placed a cigarette in her mouth and went to open the door.

Christmas looked down to where I stood. I waved three fingers at her. I wanted to get up to her or back outside and on home, somehow missing my brother.

"Well, let me guess. Another Florida Cracker," Easter said. She swung the door open wide, and with a sweeping motion of her thin, white hand made an invisible path for Willie-Bill to follow in.

All of a sudden I got a sick feeling in my stomach. And I can't tell you straight out why either. It was just so weird there, in that house. It was like Christmas and Easter, and even me and Willie-Bill, were in a movie.

The old lady came back into the foyer.

"Haven't I told you not to smoke in the house," she said to Easter. The woman made a grab at the cigarette, but Easter bent over backward till I thought her head might touch the floor.

"It's just dangling, Maude," Easter said, straightening. "I'm not planning on lighting it." Then she stepped close to Maude and I felt myself cringe. Maude didn't move anything except her eyes, which batted together, fast like she expected a slap. "Let me remind you, old woman, that you work here." Then, sure enough, she lit up the cigarette.

Maude glanced up at Christmas, who still leaned over the ledge above.

I swallowed twice.

"No smoking in the house," Maude said again. Her voice was sad sounding, and frightened, and for a brief moment it seemed so lonely that it made my heart ache.

"Are we going to read together, Maude?" Christmas asked.

"I do what I want," Easter said.

"I can see that," Maude said. "Christmas, I'm coming up in a little while. You have company." She stomped from the room, thin, wrinkled, and angry.

All this time Willie-Bill had stood quiet. Once Maude left, he let out a low whistle.

"Why, yawl have yourselves a big ol' place here," he said.

Knowing Willie-Bill like I do, I knew that he was saying something nice to Easter. But I guess she doesn't think her house is that great. She rolled her eyes so that only the whites showed.

"It's like a thimble compared to our last place," Easter said. She turned to Willie-Bill and looked him square in the eye.

"You ever swim naked?" she said.

"Naked?" Willie-Bill said. He looked like an old catfish just slung onto dry land. His mouth started flapping like he was trying to take in a breath. He probably *was* trying to take in a breath.

Easter took Willie-Bill by the arm and started to lead him toward the back of the house. "Miriam was in a movie where all she did was swim naked. That was filmed in the South. Let's go try it." Easter faked a Southern accent. It was a bad imitation.

Willie-Bill looked over at me. He's a modest guy. I couldn't imagine him jumping into a pool naked with somebody who wanted a tattoo. Or with somebody who didn't, for that matter.

"You better not," I said to him, reaching out. "Momma."

Easter gave a sharp laugh. "You let your momma make your decisions?" When she said "momma" the word had an ugly sound to it.

"Well, no," Willie-Bill said. He gave a nervous swipe to his hair.

"Then come on."

Easter disappeared, her yellow boots clicking on the stone floor.

"Willie-Bill," I said, my voice a loud whisper.

My brother turned to look at me.

"Stay here." I mouthed the words and pointed next to me.

But Willie-Bill just gave me a funny half smile, said, "Don't tell," and hurried away.

I looked back up at Christmas. Her eyebrows were knit together and she didn't appear happy.

"I'm Honey," I somehow managed to say. "That's my name."

"Well, I'm busy, Honey," Christmas said. And she turned around and left, too.

For the longest of minutes I stood in the grand foyer of the Season mansion, alone. I kept thinking maybe Christmas would come back. But she never did.

Chapter 6

A FEW DAYS LATER, WHILE I PRACTICED THE piano, our doorbell rang.

I heard Momma, barefoot, heading to the front of the house. I pounded out Chopin, in a rush to see who might be there. It wasn't often that we got visitors, not out here in the middle of nowhere. Sometimes, if someone was lost and the Sinclair green-dinosaur gas station was closed, there'd be a knock at the door. But mostly our visitors were people we planned to be here: Pop-Pop every Sunday for the after-meetings meal, Daddy's parents every third or fourth month down from Georgia, and my cousins, Cindy, Joe, and Jimmy, who showed up two weeks out of the year from Indiana to see what it was like to live out in the country.

I finished my piece and pushed in the piano bench, hoping to at least see the trunk of a car driving away. I nearly ran smack into Christmas, who Momma was leading into the room.

"Hey," she said. "I wanted to know if maybe you'd like to do something together. Maybe Rollerblade. Or ride bikes." She held up a pair of hot pink in-line skates. "You got blades?"

"Not a pair that fit," I said. "But my bike's over that-away."

We went outside, the screen door slamming behind us.

I made my way to the side of the house while Christmas tied on her skates. "This is weird," I said under my breath. "I can't believe she came over."

I pushed my bike over to where she sat on the steps.

"I'm ready," she said. "Let's get out of here."

"Your place?"

"No way," Christmas said, shaking her head so hard her hair flew out in a small, puffy circle. "Miriam is about to drive me mad." She started walking on the grassy part of our driveway, the center, where tires never hit. I pushed my bike, so I didn't get too far ahead of her.

We walked in silence, just the sound of the wheels clicking and Christmas's blades on the ground. Every once in a while I would hear the call of a whippoorwill or the cry of a mockingbird. The day was a peaceful one.

"How long have you lived here?" Christmas asked.

"Forever," I said.

"You like it?"

I thought. "I like it fine."

Off in the distance, in a huge field, I saw cows, red and white and brown lumps. I breathed deep the cooked grass smell and looked at the phlox that ran like crazy up the sweeping small hills that Christmas and I passed. "I like it real fine," I said, 'cause right at that moment, and with a promise of a whole summer waiting ahead, it was true.

"What about me?" Christmas said.

I paused to think again. "I like you fine, too."

"No," Christmas said. "I mean, do you think I'll like it here? Doesn't seem there's much to do."

We were to the highway now. We turned left.

"Well, there's not if all you're wanting is a tattoo."

"I don't want a tattoo."

"Just checking."

Christmas laughed a little. She skated up close to me and grabbed ahold of the bar on my bike. "Pull me," she said.

I stood to pedal, pushing us through the hot, heavy air of the afternoon. All the work I was doing stirred up a slight breeze. Every once in a while, Christmas pushed along. After a moment she started to sing:

> In this world of grief and pain
> In this world so full of rain
> I am touched to be with you
> To be here with you
>
> You are shelter from the night
> You keep me from the heat of day
> You make me touched to be with you
> To be here with you

The song went on and on and the voice that sang it was so sad and full and beautiful it sounded like it should be coming from anyone else but the girl skating alongside of me.

"Wow," I said, when Christmas stopped. "Where'd you learn to sing like that?"

"I was born this way," she answered.

"Born singing?"

"Yes," Christmas said. "Miriam was pregnant with me and kept hearing this funny noise coming from her belly. She went to the doctor and he told her I was humming, that I'd probably be a singer."

"And . . ." I hesitated, not knowing what to say really.

"And so I've always sung, and I write songs, too. But I never want to do anything on the stage the way Miriam wanted me to, so I haven't. And that's all there is to the story." She pointed to the field, changing the subject out from under me. "Look at that."

Close to us now were the cows, fat cows, chewing up the grass.

"Those yours, Honey?" she said.

"Naw," I said, shaking my head. "All this land belongs to a church farm. My Pop-Pop says the Mormons own it."

"Oh. You ever ride one of those things?"

"A cow?" I said. "No way."

Christmas started to slow down, slowing my bike along with her. "Let's go look at them," she said.

"All right." I pulled off the road and looked.

"I mean, let's see them up close and personal."

"How close?" I asked.

"As close as we can get," Christmas said, and she stepped off the road onto the small, sandy lip that kept the strip of blacktop from falling into the ditch. I parked my bike on the white line and followed her.

The ditch was deep, waist high, and filled with tall, dried-out grasses.

"Watch for snakes," I said, mostly to myself, but as a warning to Christmas, too.

"Okay." Christmas stepped sideways up the opposite side until she came to the flat land that is Florida. I was close on her heels. The grass made me feel itchy and hotter than I thought possible. I climbed up beside Christmas and, hanging on to the fence, looked into the great field and at the cows that were only a few yards away.

"They're beautiful," Christmas said, and her voice came out a sigh that reminded me of her song. "Think they'll come over to us?"

"I don't know," I said. "You've heard dumb as an ox, haven't you?"

"Yeah, but these are cows. Come here, baby," Christmas said.

Baby? I thought, but I said nothing.

The cow nearest us, a big red one with a white splotch on her side, looked at Christmas and me.

"Help call her over," Christmas said.

"Cow," I said in a loud voice.

The cow continued to give us the old eyeball. A big old brown eyeball, for that matter.

"Here cow-ey, cow-ey, cow-ey," Christmas said, like she was calling a kitten.

"Cow," I said again. "Cow."

The cow stared a moment more, and chewing, took a heavy step toward us.

"She's coming," Christmas said, her voice all excited.

Once the big thing got to moving it didn't look like she was gonna be able to stop once she was over to the barbed wire fence where we stood.

"*Clomp, clomp, clomp,*" said the cow's hooves on the hard ground of the field.

"Cow, stop," I said.

She didn't.

"Don't make her stop," said Christmas. "I want to ride her."

"What?" I said, my voice high with surprise. "You don't ride cows."

"Who says?" Christmas unlaced one Rollerblade.

The cow was right up to the fence now. Several others were headed our way as well.

"Oh, great," I said. "A stampede." It wasn't really, though. The cows were going so slow they weren't even raising a dust cloud. If you've watched any cowboy movies you know true stampedes have dust clouds.

"Cow," said Christmas, "I'm your friend. I'm from California. I want to ride you. I've always wanted to ride a cow. I've been on a llama and a horse and a camel, but I've never ridden anything like you. Oh, and an elephant. I've been on an elephant. I can't die until I've ridden a cow."

"You might die riding the cow," I said.

But Christmas wasn't listening. She was undoing her other Rollerblade.

The cow was right close to us now. So close I could see her nose was wet in some places and dusty in others. It popped into my mind that I was glad I didn't have to eat anything straight off the ground with only my lips and teeth to assist me.

"Help me over," Christmas said. She held her two long skate strings in her hands, knotting them together as she spoke.

At first I couldn't say anything. Then I managed to get out the words. "It's awful big."

Christmas gave me the eye, kind of like the cow had. "So?"

"So, I'm scared of it."

"Scared?" Christmas dropped her head a bit and looked at me through her bangs.

"Yeah, scared. Look how giant she is." I pointed to the cow that seemed as big around as three huge barrels.

"Elephants are bigger," Christmas said, still looking at me. "Have you ever been on an elephant?"

"Sure, at Busch Gardens. But I've never walked up to one in somebody's field and climbed aboard. Have you?"

Christmas shook her head. "Cows are bovine."

I remembered the word "bovine" from vocabulary building and enrichment. Boy, I hated that class. Seems to me the best way to teach vocabulary is to let a soul read. Of course, I might not have ever run across the word "bovine."

"That means cows are patient," Christmas said.

Now I gave Christmas a look.

"Don't you believe the dictionary?"

"What's this got to do with the dictionary?" I said, hands on my hips. Overhead a rain cloud had started gathering. It must have been coming on to three o'clock.

"I read 'bovine' in the dictionary. It means to be patient like a cow."

"Yeah. So?"

Christmas smiled. "So, I want to ride this one." And without waiting for me to help she went to squeeze between the barbed wire of the fence. It caught on her shirt, snagging a tight hold. Christmas wiggled this way and that, trying to set herself free. She only got caught tighter.

"Let me help," I said.

"Thanks," Christmas said, hunched over, her head sticking near the cow's belly, her feet on my side of the fence.

The cow sidestepped out of the way, making heavy sounds. She let out a big breath of air.

I worked at the fabric that was caught in the fence. At last Christmas was free.

"You got a hole," I told her, but she didn't seem

worried. She wasn't even listening, just bent on getting through the fence and to that cow.

The cow and its friends, who were getting closer all the time, watched Christmas. So did I. I mean, I'd never even heard of someone riding a cow before. A bull, yes. But not a cow.

Using a soft voice, almost a soothing voice, Christmas held her hand out to the cow. "I'm gonna call you Emmaline," she said. "Betsy or Elsie or Spot isn't good enough for you."

The cow lumbered back a step.

"You don't have to be afraid of me. I'm your friend."

That's when I saw the bull. He was a ways off, just a black speck in the distance. I'm not even sure how I knew he was a bull. My guts just told me so. "I think you better get this ride over with," I said.

Christmas touched the cow on the neck, her hand seeming to shrink in size as she caressed the red color there.

Still the bull was too far away for me to see clearly, but there was one thing I knew. He was headed in our direction. He didn't seem to be going too fast, but he was for sure coming to see what it was the rest of the cows were gawking at.

Christmas put one arm over the cow's neck and the next thing I knew she was up, almost without a problem. It's true she did some scrambling, her feet climbing up the side of the rounded body. But then she was sitting high up in the saddle. Okay, there was no saddle, but you know what I mean. Leaning forward, Christmas draped the laces around the cow's neck.

"It's too short," I said. "It looks like a necklace."

"I'll be okay without it," Christmas said. Then she started singing. "Whoopie-tie-hie-ho get along little doggie." She nudged the cow with her socked foot.

That's when I saw that the black beast moving toward us really *was* a bull.

The cow looked back a little at Christmas then took a step or two.

"I'm doing something that I wondered if I'd ever have time to do," Christmas said.

"Well," I said. "I'm thinking you're running out of time."

The bull had stopped moving. Probably, if he'd been a little more human, he'd have dropped his mouth open in surprise to see a small, short-haired girl on top of one of his cows. I know my mouth was open.

"He's getting closer."

"Gid-yap, Ol' Emmaline," Christmas said, then she threw back her head and started singing a song that Elvis Presley used to sing. The one about the blue suede shoes. I'm not sure why she sang it, it didn't really fit the mood of things, especially with that bull coming up to see what was going on.

He was pretty close now. Not Elvis Presley, the bull. So close I could see that he didn't look friendly, not one little bit. It seemed to me that if the Mormon Church was going to have a bull in their pasture they should have chosen a friendly one.

"You better get off that cow and head on back to safety." That's what I tried to say when the bull lowered his head and began to trot in our direction. I think the only sound that came out was kind of garbled and spitty, "Arrggh!"

The cow moved a little this way and that and Christmas swayed on top of it, singing something about a jailhouse rock.

Oh no, I thought. The bull had picked up speed. "Get off," I wanted to say. "Get out." But my jaw just chomped up and down.

Now the bull ran at full speed.

It was me that saved Christmas's life. For some reason she looked in my direction and I managed to raise a shaking arm and point.

She jumped off the cow and took a few galloping steps toward the fence and safety. The bull kept coming and then I realized *I* was the only soul he noticed, not Christmas, who rolled on the ground, trying to get clear of cow feet that moved every which way and free of the barbed wire.

I backed up, fast, wondering if that rickety old fence would hold when the bull tried to bust through. I hoped he would miss goring me with his horns and hoped he wouldn't try to stomp my guts out.

"Aaaah," I said, and fell backward into the ditch.

Christmas leaped down beside me, free, and with only a few new holes in her shirt. She crawled over to where I lay, flat on my back, my legs moving like I was running.

"Ha ha," she said in my face, laughing so hard that at first I was angry.

"You almost got me killed," I said, my voice found and my legs still except for shaking.

Tears ran down Christmas's face. "If you could have only seen your expression. Miriam has been trying for years to get real fear on her face. She can't do it, not like what you just did."

Christmas dropped her head onto her arm and screeched with laughter.

"Maybe your momma needs to be chased down by a Mormon bull and then fall into a ditch backward," I said. I felt a little bent out of shape. Riding the cow had not been my idea and I could have fallen into a nest of snakes or broken my back or both.

Christmas laughed even harder.

Things started getting funny once I checked myself out and saw I had no injuries. I laughed in the ditch, covered in prickly, itchy weeds, remembering Christmas swaying on the cow. Then watching her running and rolling and then me looking at nothing but beautiful blue sky filling up with thunderclouds.

"Weren't you scared?" I said to Christmas as we walked toward home. I pushed my bike. Christmas carried her skates; she'd left her laces around the cow's neck. Some farmer was going to be surprised.

"I'm not scared of anything," Christmas said. "And you shouldn't be neither, Honey."

"I'm scared of plenty."

"Of what?"

"Dying," I said. I left out the getting saved part. Christmas looked at me.

"Don't tell anybody that," she said. "You don't want them to know where they can hurt you. Your being afraid gives other people that chance."

We said good-bye halfway between her driveway and mine. As I started off, biking the short distance home, I thought about what I was afraid of: living in a family of people who were all saved except for me.

You see, I respect a lot of what Pop-Pop says in his preaching. Like him teaching me to be good so I can live with God again. But some things that Pop-Pop talks about scare the hell outta me and that's just putting it blunt. Like when Jesus comes back again.

According to Pop-Pop we have to be prepared. And part of that being prepared is getting saved. The thing I can't do.

I'm worried. Does God really have angels taking notes about everything I do, like the song says? Just how bad is bad? I mean, I don't kill people or drink alcohol or steal. But I do bug Willie-Bill half to death. I help Momma out as much as I can, but sometimes I think if I see Taylor wink at me one more time he'd look better in an eye patch.

I'm confused and I'm worried and I'm not real sure where the answers are. That's just how it is.

Chapter 7

HAVE YOU EVER NOTICED LAUGHING YOUR guts out with someone makes them a friend? At least that's the way it happened with Christmas and me. A couple of days later, early in the morning, when I still sat at the table in my jammies, a knock sounded.

"I'll get it," Willie-Bill said, and in Eeyore-like slow motion he got up and started to the front door. Momma was dishing out French toast for me, fat pieces of bread thick with eggs and vanilla. She topped each with a generous dollop of homemade whipped cream and then fresh-made strawberry syrup.

When I looked up, there in the hallway stood Christmas.

"Honey," she said.

My face broke wide open with a smile. "Hey," I said.

Momma raised her eyebrows at me. The two of us hadn't talked about the cow-riding incident. I'd only told her that I liked Christmas and that I thought we might be friends.

Now I grinned at my mother.

"Will you join us, Christmas?" Momma didn't even wait for an answer, but sat Christmas down next to me and gave her a bright blue plate filled up with French toast and cubed melon and crispy bacon.

"Wow," Christmas whispered when Momma handed her a glass of juice. "You eat this way all the time?"

I grinned, my mouth full of food. "Every meal."

"I only get yogurt," Christmas said. She frowned. "Low fat." Then she looked at me and for some reason we laughed loud together. Maybe it was the whipped cream or maybe the low fat idea. Or maybe it was the cow and the bull riding into our memories. Whatever, we laughed until Momma said, "Girls, eat." Then we giggled the rest of breakfast.

"Now what?" Christmas said after we'd cleared the table. We were in my room and Christmas peered out my west window.

"The day is ours," I said.

"What's that shiny place over there?"

I looked out past the open fields to a stand of trees where light shimmered.

"A lake."

Christmas turned to me. "A lake? Have you ever been there?"

"Are you kidding? I used to go out there all the time. It's part of our property."

"That's where I want to go now."

"Easy. Let's go get Momma to pack us a lunch then head on out there."

"All right," said Christmas.

And we were off.

The lake was at least a mile away. By the time we started the sun was already hot in the sky. We walked without talking, and I soaked up all the good feelings that seemed to dance through my head: the weather, the prospects of lunch outdoors, and a friend.

At long last Christmas and I stood on the edge of the lake. It wasn't that big, maybe two or three acres. But I knew from experience it was cool from the springs that fed it and because of the trees that shaded it.

"This is great," Christmas said. She breathed a big sigh, like maybe she felt as satisfied as I did with the beginnings of our day.

"Yeah," I said. "Me and Taylor and Willie-Bill, we used to come here all the time. Momma never knew. She doesn't like me in the water unless there's an adult nearby." Boy, that's the truth. Why, she'd have thrown a conniption fit if she had known that we would swim here.

"How come?" Christmas was stripping off her shoes and socks. I was barefoot already.

Trees crowded close to the edge of the lake, at least on the side where we stood.

"You know. Snakes. Drowning. Natural disasters. The things mommas worry about." I climbed up onto a cypress tree root that lifted from the moist ground like an ancient finger. After a moment, I sat to take a rest. Stretching my foot out, I touched the warm water with the tip of one toe.

"Your mother worries about those kinds of things?" Christmas parked her shoes next to where I dropped my backpack.

"Sure," I said. "And lots of other stuff."

"Like what?"

I thought. "Gangs, the conditions of the world, botulism, rattlers, drugs, hardening of the arteries, high blood pressure, killers. The list is endless."

"Is that why you live in the middle of nowhere?" Christmas sat down next to me. Sweat had trickled down the sides of her face and dried. I could see the leftover paths.

I shrugged. "Maybe," I said. "Why are you here? Is your momma afraid of something?"

"Just what Easter might do," Christmas said. "Let's swim."

There's something creepy about swimming in some Florida lakes. Don't get me wrong. I love swimming. But this lake has always looked different. Dark. Now I couldn't see a white bottom anywhere, not even close to the shore. Mud had covered things like a brown, hairy carpet.

"Swim?" I said.

"Yeah."

Minnows nibbled at my feet when I stepped in a bit farther.

"This is gonna ruin our clothes," I said.

"So?" Christmas said.

"Momma," I started, then I stopped. "Okay."

"And we'll swim in our underwear," Christmas said, stripping off her shorts and then her shirt. She wore a shiny yellow bra covered in what looked to be rose blossoms.

"Underwear?" I said. My stomach flipped at the thought. Why, the only person who ever saw me in my underwear was Momma and that was just when I was a little girl.

"Our goal is to get to the other side of the lake without getting our clothes wet and eat lunch over there." Christmas folded her clothing into a small, neat pile while she spoke.

"Good goal," I said. And all of a sudden it was. I took off my shorts and T-shirt. I felt a little uncomfortable when Christmas eyeballed my Cinderella training bra.

"We need to take care of that old thing," she said, motioning to my Disney underwear, and then she was in the water, walking toward the opposite shore.

I stuffed my clothes into my backpack and followed Christmas. "Wait for me."

She took a step back. Her legs were painted dark from the mud.

"Let's hope there aren't any leeches out here," I said, grinning.

"Or swamp things," Christmas said.

"Or creatures from any black lagoons."

"Or any killers."

"Or hardened arteries." I laughed as the water rose high on my belly.

"What in the world is the ground made from?" Christmas asked. "It feels like poop."

"Yuck," I hollered. My voice screeched across the lake and got swallowed up in the trees across from us. "How do you know what poop feels like?" I started laughing. The water went from warm to cool, getting even cooler in some places.

Christmas laughed, too. "I don't," she said and her voice was a screech, too. "But I have *seen* it."

By now we were up to our necks. I balanced the backpack on my head. Christmas did the same with her clothes. The lumpy, mushy floor of the lake was getting harder to reach.

"We're gonna have to dog-paddle," I said, bouncing on tiptoes. My hair floated out in the water, catching glimmers of a high-noon sun. Christmas's hair was just starting to get wet because it was so short.

Her mouth and nose went under a little. Pursing her lips like a fountain, Christmas sprayed a silver arc of water into the air.

And then we were dog-paddling along, clothes and backpacks on our heads, trying to keep our noses above the water. Laughing was dangerous, but I couldn't help it. My voice was low and flat sounding. I floated out onto my back, only to start sinking when I tried to keep lunch from getting wet.

"Whose idea was this anyway?" Christmas asked.

"Not mine," I said. I was tired, my hair soaked from going under. I tried not to think how deep the lake might be, or what might be hiding out under our kicking feet.

"Not too much farther," Christmas said. I glanced at her. Her cheeks were pink from swimming one-handed.

I laughed again. We still had a long way to go.

"Don't talk," I said. "You're wearing me out." I giggled through my nose, snorting really.

Christmas was intent on the trek. Her nostrils flared, which made me laugh again.

"Sorry," I said, when she glared at me.

"I don't feel like drowning in an unknown lake," she said between gritted teeth. "No more laughing or talking. Or snorting."

She was serious.

"I don't want to drown either," I said, mumbling. But I was quiet after that, in case there was a chance for it. Drowning, I mean.

I tried not to think of all the things Momma had warned me about. Alligators, moccasins, and quicksand. I just paddled, not caring after a while if everything in the backpack, including my clothes, sunk into the bottomless pit of lake below me.

At last the far side came nearer and we were walking on poopy ground again. There was no real shore, so when we were waist deep in the water I tried talking to Christmas.

"Now that we're not going to drown," I said, "I think we should wait one second before going on." Water dripped off my Cinderella bra. Every hair that I could see on my body was coated with dark brown mud.

Christmas turned to me. "Whew," she said. "That was hard." She grinned.

"We made it though."

She took a step forward. And I reached out to stop her. My hand wiped a clean place on her skin.

"Really, Christmas," I said. "There could be snakes out here. Or 'gators."

Christmas's eyes got a little wider.

"So I think we should run as fast as hell," I said. "And get into the safety of the woods."

"Where all the killers are hiding."

I laughed. "Right," I said. Then, "One, two, three, go!"

We ran.

Excitement seemed to shoot from my guts out into my fingers and hands and even to the roots of my hair. Was one of Momma's perverts watching us? I wondered. I let out a scream, just for the fun of it.

Christmas screamed, too.

I screamed louder, scared now.

"What?" Christmas's voice was a yell.

On we ran, through the lumpy mud, through the tall reeds on the shoreline, past the marshy ground, on until we were on dry, solid earth. The whole time we screamed. My heart pumped hard. In our underwear we ran, coated in brown like we had been dipped in chocolate.

"What, what, what?" Christmas hollered, and her voice got caught up in the trees and weeds. A hidden squirrel scolded us.

"Nothing," I shouted back, still frightened. I glanced around, looking for snakes and alligators, but there were none to be found.

"Nothing?" she asked, then she laughed.

Relief seemed to calm me. "Whoo hoo," I called out to the squirrel that got quiet then chattered all the more. I did a few steps from tap class, swinging the backpack in front of me, water streaming out of my hair and into my eyes and down my face.

Christmas threw back her head and started singing a made-up song. "We made it, we're not dead. We made it, now we can eat lunch. Yahoo." She danced in her under-wear, swinging her shirt around in one hand and her shorts around in the other. I danced with her, wondering what Mr. Walt Disney might think of Cinderella moving the way she was.

I got dressed as soon as my skin had dried off a little. "Let's eat in the sun," I said.

"My clothes are wet," Christmas said. She pulled her shorts onto dirty legs.

"So are mine," I said. "But lunch was in plastic bags, so that's safe."

We found a grassy place to sit, partway in the sun and in the shade, too. I pulled the food out, setting the fruit and sandwiches and fresh cookies on the ground in front of us. Water had beaded up on the Baggies, but the food was dry. And so were the napkins. Even the milk was cold in its containers.

"Let's eat," I said, after saying a blessing in my heart.

"Then we can discuss that little Cinderella training bra of yours," Christmas said with a smile.

Chapter 8

ONE AFTERNOON, WHILE WE SAT IN MY OLD tree house, I got up all my courage and asked Christmas about her father. I just had to know about the tattoos. I couldn't imagine a man covered in rabbits, though I did see a guy tattooed with different Disney characters once on television.

"Tattoos?" Christmas asked, and her voice sounded funny. "What makes you think he has tattoos?"

"Easter told me that he did. She said he's covered in rabbits." I thought Christmas would laugh, but she didn't. Instead she got a sneer on her face that didn't look like it would ever go away.

"She's a liar. I mean, worse than anyone I know. Worse than Miriam even."

We were eating lunch, a special salad that Momma had mixed up for us in a Tupperware container. She'd sent along a little note taped to the plastic lid. It said: *Have a good day, girls. Honey, I do love you, Momma.* I dished us big bowls full of salad that had raisins and bits of bacon and broccoli in it.

"Your mother lies, too?" It seemed more possible, suddenly, for my father to be covered with rabbits than for my mother to lie.

"All the time. It's part of being an actress. At least it's part of her being an actress."

"Gah," I said. "I think I'd hate that."

Christmas shrugged. "It's my life." Her voice sounded so matter-of-fact that I was surprised. This girl had ridden a cow only a few days before and had told me never to admit being afraid. She had gone swimming across a bottomless pit. And here she was sounding almost like she had given up over things. "What can I do about it anyway?"

"Nothing, I guess." And then I could see the reason maybe Christmas sounded like it was better to give up than to care. She couldn't make her momma do or be different than she was.

"Our father is a stunt man. That's how Miriam met him, on one of her movies. They lived together awhile, then Miriam got pregnant. Then they got married. Then she decided she wanted another baby. Then she decided she hated my dad, so they got a divorce. I get to see him sometimes. I was supposed to spend the summer with him. But then you and I got to know each other and so I told him I'd come and visit on my namesake."

"What do you mean, your namesake?"

"I told him I'd come for Christmas."

"Don't you want to see him now?"

Christmas shrugged again. "Not really. I used to want

to, you know, when I was younger. But I don't see him that often, so it doesn't bother me anymore. Anyway, there was a chance to get to know you. So here I am." Christmas held her hands out, one with a fork, one with her plate.

Things were getting stranger all the time. Would I give up a summer with my dad to spend it with someone who *might* be a friend?

"Your house is better than mine," she said after a bit of being quiet. "This tree house is better than that place we live in."

"How can you say that, Christmas?" I said. In my head I could see the swimming pool reflecting light in my eyes. Clean water, no mud involved. "Yours must have cost an American Van Line truckload of money to build. How can you say it's not fantastic?"

"It doesn't have all that I want."

"You're kidding?" Surprise made my voice go all high and squeaky.

Christmas stood up and went to look out a curtained window. Below us was the ant bed, big and always seeming alive except at night or when the weather turned bitter or rainy. If you aimed just right you could drop bits of leftovers there and in the next few hours the ants would clean it all up.

"I want a tree house just like this, with a friend in it, just like you. I want a note from my mother. One that she writes because she means it and not for show."

She sat next to me and we started eating again. "You

have about everything worth anything, Honey," Christmas said.

"Naw, I don't."

"Sure you do." Christmas ate the whole time she spoke, stuffing her mouth full of salad, really enjoying the food. For some reason, watching her eat made everything taste better, like maybe I hadn't realized how good it was.

"Tell me," I said. "What do I have that you don't?"

Christmas smacked her lips together. "This salad."

"What? This ol' stuff? Momma makes it all the time. She even sells it at the diner."

"I know. Miriam has sent our chauffeur out to get some."

I shrugged my shoulders like, See, you can buy what I have.

Christmas leaned toward me. "But your mother makes it for you. *Makes* it. Miriam wouldn't even think of walking into our kitchen unless she wanted to boss someone in there around. Miriam wouldn't *make* it for me."

"She doesn't have to, Christmas. She can hire someone to do it for her."

"Don't you see the difference?"

I didn't really. I mean, how would you feel with so much money you could buy anything you wanted? Or anything you didn't want, for that matter.

Christmas took a forkful of food and chewed it up slow. Then she said, "Your mother does it because she loves you. Mine doesn't." It was a simple statement, just like that.

"Miriam loves you," I said, but I wasn't real sure I believed it. I had seen Miriam Season only the one time in our diner and it had seemed then that she was busy showing off her own self. And proof lived right next door to me that a momma sometimes doesn't do right by her kid. Taylor.

Christmas acted like what I had said was the most ridiculous thing ever. She rolled her eyes around her head a couple of times. "Yeah, she loves me all right." She paused a moment, then said, "What I want is a tree house like this."

"You can build one," I said.

"Did you build this?"

"Uh-uh." I shook my head no.

"Who did?"

I was slow to answer 'cause I knew what I was stepping into before I got there. "My daddy did it when we first moved out here."

Christmas gave me a look like, Need I go on? I gave her a weak grin.

"My father has never built anything for me," she said after a minute. "And now, even if he wanted to, I don't think Miriam would let him. Bad karma, having him around." Christmas said this last thing like she was Miriam herself. She did a pretty good imitation.

"Isn't there anybody for you?"

"I do have Maude," Christmas said. "She's my nanny. I can't ever remember her not being with me."

There was nothing I could say. No words seemed right.

"Look, we got a summer," I said finally. "It wouldn't be the same, but why don't we build a tree house for you? You got any good trees out at your place?"

Christmas thought a second. "There's a monster one at the back of the property."

"Are there any low limbs?"

She nodded. "I think so. I haven't really gone out and looked at it."

"Well it sounds to me that would be a perfect place. You want to try?"

Christmas smiled. "You mean it?" she said. "Would you really help me do that?"

"Sure," I said. "We'd need some scrap lumber. But I got nails and a couple of hammers that Daddy would let us use."

Christmas climbed out of the tree house to go talk to Miriam and see if it would be okay. I followed her down, then walked her and her bike to the end of my long driveway. We stopped by the diner.

"Do you think your mother would make us more of that salad for our lunches?" Christmas said.

"I'm thinking so," I said.

And we separated for that day.

"Family prayer in ten minutes," I heard Momma call as I watched Christmas pedal herself home on her bicycle.

Momma's voice was thin and distant, barely floating its way to where I was.

The sun was sinking fast and dragonflies darted this way and that, looking for a meal.

"I'm coming," I called, not sure if my voice would stretch all the way to the house. I started home, jogging and thinking.

"Dear Heavenly Father," I said. "Thank you, thank you, thank you that my momma loves me."

The thought made me want to run and wrap my arms around her tight. "And thank you that Christmas came."

That evening after our family time together, I climbed into bed and pulled the covers up to my chin. Outside, heat lightning played across the sky and faraway thunder rumbled, rolling closer.

I started thinking about Christmas. She never invited me to her house and I was dying to go see it. I wanted to see her room. Was her bed as big as she said? Did she really have a refrigerator in her bathroom area and her own private Jacuzzi bathtub and deck?

I wanted to sneak into Easter's room. Was it really painted blacker than the clothes she wore? Did she really hide bottles of alcohol that Miriam pretended not to know about and that even Willie-Bill had mentioned? I wanted to see if it was possible to cannonball into the pool from her balcony.

And I wanted to get to know their nanny, the front door answerer, who had seemed so sad that first day.

But Christmas never let me in that far.

I kept thinking, though I was getting sleepy.

What about Momma? Did she protect me like Christmas said? She certainly did things for me that Miriam Season didn't do for her daughters. Was it good or bad? Parents were supposed to protect their kids, weren't they? I was sure there was a law that said something like that somewhere. Daddy would know.

I went to sleep at last, with the thunder echoing in my head and feeling safe with the thought Daddy had answers and Momma cared.

Chapter 9

THE NEXT DAY CHRISTMAS AND I WENT LOOK-ing for scrap lumber around my place, out in our old barn, and collecting nails and tools to work with. We came up with six two-by-fours and four huge pieces of plywood. One was shaped like the state of Utah. We carried this all down to the diner and stacked it against the wall. I was sweating good when we set down the last piece.

"We've got a long way to go to get this to your place," I said, wiping my brow on the hem of my T-shirt. "And I can't think of how to get this there without carrying it." Both Momma and Daddy had left to go shopping at the Farmers' Market in Edgewater. Then they were shopping for basic home and diner food necessities. Last of all they would be checking in on Pop-Pop, then coming home. Willie-Bill was somewhere in the house.

"What about him?" Christmas asked, and she pointed over my shoulder toward the Sinclair green-dinosaur gas station.

I turned around. There was Taylor, stacking tires in

front of an oily garbage can. He wore blue jeans and a used-to-be white T-shirt made greasy with handprints. "What *about* him?" I said.

"He looks like he could lug lumber anywhere." Christmas wiggled her eyebrows at me, up and down, up and down.

"Probably he could," I said. "But are you sure you wanna ask him?"

"I don't want to ask him. I thought maybe you could. You know him, don't you?"

"Yeah. But naw," I said. "I don't think so."

Christmas grabbed a piece of two-by-four. "Get the other end, then," she said.

I gave Taylor the old eyeball. I thought of the long, hot, sweaty walk to Christmas's house and all the trips we'd have to make. I looked back at Taylor again and let out a sigh. "Let's go talk to him," I said.

Christmas let the board go with a smack and the two of us started over. By now Taylor was moving the tires again, to a different position in front of another garbage can.

In a moment we stood under the roof that shaded the four gas pumps from the heavy sun.

"Hey," I said.

Taylor jumped. "Honey," he said. "Hey." A big ol' smile went across his face like he hadn't seen me in a million years or something. Truth be told, he'd spent the morning staring at me over breakfast. Then he worked with Willie-Bill on a Klingon battle cruiser. You know, a Star Trek model. "Whatchu doing here?"

"I need a couple of tires, Taylor," I said.

"Zat so? You're such a kidder, Honey." Taylor grinned at me, then extended his hand to Christmas. "I'm Taylor Hiatt. My daddy owns this place. I'm gonna be a writer."

Christmas reached out in slow motion and took Taylor's hand. He pumped it up and down. "I see you're already good friends with Honey," he said. "Isn't she great?"

"Taylor," I said, knocking their hands apart. An unexpected feeling of jealousy filled up my chest. It made me feel angry. "We need your help and we haven't got all day to hear your song-and-dance routine. Now listen to me."

"Any old time, you know I will," Taylor said, fixing his big eyes onto mine. "How can I be of service?"

I heaved another sigh, glanced at Christmas with a, Are you sure you wanna do this? look, and said, "We need you to carry some boards with us."

"What boards?"

"Some that we found."

"What are they for?"

"Look," I said, "can you help or not?"

"Sure. Let me tell Daddy."

Taylor was gone a little bit and the next thing we knew Lyman Hiatt stuck his head out the garage part of the gas station. "Be back as soon as you can, kid. In case I need you."

"Yessir. I'll be back shortly," Taylor said. "Just let me help these young ladies." He grinned right in my face. I wrinkled my nose at the gassy, oily smell that floated around Taylor. Christmas stood quiet.

"This way," I said.

We started to the piled-up lumber.

"Where's this all going?" Taylor said when we arrived at the wood.

"My house," Christmas said.

Taylor gazed at her a moment, then looked at me. "There's a lot of stuff here," he said. "I think we gonna need Billy's help."

I snorted. "Well, if you find the magic button that makes that happen, let me know. Willie-Bill complains about having to chew and swallow."

Taylor laughed. "I'll go call him."

The sun poured down, hot and heavy. On the gravelly sand of the driveway, bull ants crawled around, working together to carry an almost dead grasshopper down their hole.

I kicked at the ground. "Great," I said. "Now we got the biggest complainer in all the land might be coming to work with us."

"It won't be as hard," Christmas said. "Not with four of us doing it."

She came over to me and threw a hot arm on my shoulder. "We'll carry the boards over, then we'll send them on their way. Deal?"

"Okay, deal."

It was then that I heard the truck backfire. When I looked over my shoulder, I saw Taylor sitting up behind the wheel of his daddy's old red pickup.

"Let's go," he said.

Chapter 10

"A TRUCK!" CHRISTMAS SAID. "THINGS ARE getting better and better."

"I don't know about that. He doesn't have a license," I said, throwing a thumb at Taylor. "Whatchu doing?" I said to Willie-Bill, who sat in the cab.

"Nothing."

"I'm surprised," I said.

"What's Christmas doing here?" he asked.

"We're hauling some stuff."

"To where?"

"Her place."

"You mean we're going over there?" Willie-Bill wiped his hand over his upper lip. "Taylor didn't tell me that."

"Where'd you get the truck?" I heard Christmas say. I went over to her side. She gave me a fat smile.

"My daddy owns the gas station," Taylor said, throwing pieces of wood into the back of the truck. Christmas helped.

"Your point?" I said, standing with my hands on my hips.

"All gas station attendants know how to drive, Honey."

The last of the wood was in the bed of the truck now. I tossed in the hammers and the bag of nails.

"Let's go," Taylor said. Christmas ran to where Willie-Bill sat. "Scoot over," I heard her say.

Now I crossed my arms in front of my chest. "How long you been driving?"

"Since before I was born." Taylor smiled at me. His white teeth seemed to shine in the sun. His dark hair hung in his eyes.

"Yeah. Does your daddy know about this?"

"Of course. You know me good enough to know I wouldn't do something that Daddy wouldn't approve of." Taylor leaned close. "He approves of you, Honey."

"Oh."

"One day," Taylor said, "one day you'll love me back."

Willie-Bill let out a guffaw.

"Good grief, Taylor Hiatt," I said. My face burned. Why did he have to say things in front of other people? "Let's go."

I climbed in the cab next to Christmas.

"He likes you," she whispered.

I closed my eyes tight.

Taylor put the truck in gear. There was a terrible scrunching noise.

"Grind me a pound while you're at it," Willie-Bill said, as we pulled out onto the highway.

Taylor laughed. He's always laughing at everything my brother says.

"Scoot over." I slapped at Willie-Bill's leg. "You got more room than all three of us put together."

Willie-Bill sat up a little straighter and moved over half an inch. "Think Easter's at home?"

"If she is," I said, "she'll run when she sees you pull in the yard."

Taylor shifted the truck into second. The gears seemed to cry out in pain. We all four jerked toward the windshield.

"You're making us all suffer," I said to Taylor. "Including your daddy's truck."

"Christmas," Willie-Bill said, "you think Easter's home?"

"Maybe," Christmas said. "Or at counseling. Or rehab."

Willie-Bill straightened up even more. He peered out the glass. "Better shift gears, Hiatt, or we ain't ever getting there."

Taylor chuckled again.

"You sure your daddy knows we got this truck?"

"Now, Honey," Taylor said, and gazed over at me.

"Keep your eyes on the road," I said.

"Shift," Willie-Bill said.

The truck ground out a protest.

Christmas giggled. "Or she could still be in bed."

"Maybe you should use the clutch," I said. "At least

that's what Momma does when she drives. Pushes in the clutch."

"I'm using the clutch."

"Doesn't sound like it."

"Put on the gas and you may get us up to fourth gear."

"Keep your eyes steady on the road. Don't look at me. Watch the ditch."

"She could be out swimming."

"Think I could swim with her?"

"Stay on this side of the road, Taylor."

"Maybe, if she's at the pool."

"Quit being a backseat driver, Honey."

"I hope she's out there."

"Now you're too far over. Now you're in the grass. Now you're getting close to the ditch."

"Open up the wing window," Christmas said. "B.O. is about to drive me out of here."

"At least something's being driven," I said.

"Now, Honey," Taylor said.

"The turn's right up there," Willie-Bill said.

"I'm scared for my life," I said. I covered my nose and mouth with one hand and pointed with the other. "Watch out for that mailbox. It cost more than your daddy's gas station."

Taylor spun the wheel, big and stained dark from age and dirt, steering the truck into the driveway, just missing the mailbox.

"Whoa," I said. I felt a laugh starting up inside.

"Speed it up some," Willie-Bill said.

A bit of a giggle busted out of me.

Christmas's house sat fat and red on the built-up hill in front of us. I closed my eyes as we bumped off the driveway for a moment. The truck heaved up into the air, then stalled. I heard the wood and hammers and nails all clatter behind us.

My giggle changed into a laugh.

"You're parked on gardenia bushes," Christmas said. I could hear a smile in her voice.

An oily odor came in through the window, then the faint fragrance of flowers. I opened my eyes.

"I sure do love the smell of gardenias," I said, between laughs.

"Me, too," Christmas said. She was laughing now.

But neither Taylor nor Willie-Bill was. In fact Willie-Bill was rocking like maybe his body movement could get the truck up the steep driveway. "Start the truck," he said, staring out the window, up toward The Mansion. "Let's get going."

Taylor's face was all red. "I'm real sorry about the bushes."

"That's okay," Christmas said, her voice full of laughter. "Miriam can buy some more."

Taylor went to start the truck. We jerked forward and I wondered if Daddy could handle whiplash victims in a court of law.

"Oops," Taylor said. His face turned redder. He

looked at the three of us. "I'm not real good at going up hills."

"Could have fooled me," I said.

The truck stalled and we started rolling backward.

"Stop laughing, Honey," Taylor said, braking and snapping us all toward the windshield.

"You two are hurting my head." Willie-Bill wiggled a finger in his ear like maybe he was cleaning it out.

Taylor jerked the truck all the way up Christmas's long driveway. Now everybody looked pretty happy. Christmas was grinning because the wood was getting closer to the old oak tree. Willie-Bill was grinning 'cause he was getting closer to Easter. Taylor was grinning 'cause he was getting closer to turning off the engine.

"Where do you want me to stop?" Taylor said.

We sat in the huge concrete parking area just this side of the garages. The truck idled, shaking a little, like maybe it was scared from the driving ordeal it had just been through.

"I'm out right here," Willie-Bill said. I could see him eyeing the pool, though there wasn't anyone swimming. He climbed past Christmas and me, perfuming the air with the smell of B.O.

"Don't get too close to her, Willie-Bill," I said, waving my hand in front of my nose. "Friend to friend advice."

"Easter won't mind," Christmas said. "She doesn't believe in bathing. She says it's not natural."

Willie-Bill slammed the door, nearly mashing the surprised look off my face. Bathing wasn't natural but all that black was? I'd never learn.

"Where to?" Taylor said.

"There." Christmas pointed over the well-groomed lawn, all the way to where the woods began. There stood an old oak, green leaves shimmering in the light. The branches swooped down toward the earth, casting shade on the far grass. It was beautiful. The perfect tree for a tree house.

"I don't see a road," Taylor said.

"Just make your own," Christmas said.

"What?" Taylor said.

"Do you think that's a good idea?" I said. "My momma would be bent outta shape if we went driving across her yard."

Christmas nodded, waving her arm forward. "She won't even notice. Go ahead, Taylor. It will save us the energy of hauling everything over."

"Did you ask her, Christmas?"

She shook her head no. "Miriam was too busy to talk. Wagons ho, Taylor Hiatt."

"Okay," Taylor said, and ground out first gear. We started slowlike across the backyard. I looked behind us. There were tire prints, the grass left bent because of the truck, but nothing got torn up.

"Watch out for the tree," I said, after a minute or two of driving.

"I am, Honey."

"Are you planning to stop?"

"Yes, Honey."

Taylor grabbed at the wheel with one hand and the shifter knob with the other. He pumped wild with his clutch foot and for some reason pushed in the gas at the same time. The truck picked up speed and slowed down, screaming when the clutch was in. Picked up speed. Slowed down. Screamed when the clutch was in.

"You're getting awful close." My voice was loud.

"She's right," Christmas said.

Wham! We hit the tree. The truck coughed and died. I felt all the blood drain from my face. The leaves shook in the tree. A few floated down around us.

"Taylor," I said.

"Don't holler at me, Honey. It only makes me nervous."

"You hit the tree."

"I said don't yell at me." Taylor rested his forehead on the steering wheel. I could see the back of his neck and at least one ear was red.

We sat in the cab, all quiet. At last Christmas said, "I'll check for damages."

I climbed out and Christmas followed. We went to the front of the truck.

Taylor came after us. I noticed he was walking all slumped over.

"Just a small dent, Taylor," Christmas said.

He eyed the bumper.

"And you've knocked off only a little bark."

"It's not too bad," Taylor said.

"Then let's get a move on," I said.

Me and Christmas started hauling our finds from the bed of the truck. We stacked everything in a neat pile beneath a low limb.

"A tree house?" Taylor said. "So that's it."

Christmas nodded. "Isn't it going to be wonderful?" I thought her face might split wide open she was so happy.

I pulled myself up onto the lowest limb, then balancing myself with my arms stretched out T-shaped, made my way to the next limb, going higher and higher into the tree.

"This is great," I said. I could see through the leaves to where Christmas and Taylor stood below. "You're gonna have one fantastic place here."

"There's not enough wood," Taylor said.

"Yeah," Christmas said, following me up the tree.

"We know that," I said.

"You're gonna need a lot more. Just for the basics." Taylor swung himself up, too.

"Don't you hear your daddy calling, Taylor?" I said.

"Now, Honey," he said. "Let me just talk to you a minute. Then I'll go on home." He settled himself on a low branch and gazed at us. "Are you wanting just a flat something or other up here?"

"No," Christmas said. "I want something nice. Like what Honey has."

Taylor gave a low whistle. "You're gonna need a lot more material than that little pile down there."

"Wait, wait, wait," I said. I could see where this conversation was headed.

"Don't worry, Honey," Taylor said. "I'm not going where I'm not invited." His voice was sharp. "You been mean to me all day. I'll say this thing only 'cause I like Christmas and I want to help her. Then I'll leave."

My mouth dropped open. Taylor had never spoken to me that way. It stung a little. And so did the thought of him liking her.

"Christmas," he said, making a point to look just at her. "I can help you, if you want. I have all the lumber you'll need in the storage shed back behind my daddy's gas station."

My stung feelings were healed up and haired over just like that.

"You do?" we both said at the same time.

"I'm not talking to you, Honey," Taylor said, giving me the evil eye. "This is for Christmas to decide." He turned his attention to her again.

"You got everything?" Christmas said.

"A whole store of it," Taylor said.

Christmas grinned at Taylor. "Let me talk it over with my friend," she said.

Little bits of sun squeezed past the leaves. The light seemed to dance in the air around us. I could hear a mockingbird calling from somewhere not too far away.

Taylor jumped off the limb and started for the truck.

"What do you think?" Christmas said.

I squinted my eyes at Taylor's back and glared at him.

How could I tell her I didn't want Taylor too poked in where me and Christmas were?

"I don't know," I said. "I didn't think he was nice."

"Nicer than you've been to him today."

Had I been unkind? "Hey," I said. "I thought you were my friend."

"Your best friend," Christmas said.

Christmas's words were a comfort. She was my best friend. She'd said it. "He just gets on my nerves something fierce," I said.

"But he's not a bad guy. And he can help us."

"You're right." I felt a twinge of guilt press in my heart. I tried to ignore it.

"Should we let him?" Christmas was smiling to beat the band now.

I nodded. "As long as he doesn't try to help us build it."

"It's a deal," Christmas said.

We spent the rest of the afternoon moving the wood and materials over from the old storage shed in the back of the Sinclair green-dinosaur gas station. Taylor's daddy let him help since the day was way slow and his normal chores were done.

It wasn't till right before dinner that me and Taylor started for home.

We both sat quiet in the truck, making our slow way back, Taylor shifting and steering like there was nothing more important in the world than getting me outta his truck. We drove down the driveway in a jerky stop-and-go sort of way. When we passed the gardenia bushes I noticed they looked like the life had been squished out of them. I almost got the giggles, but I smothered the urge.

All the way home we were silent.

At last Taylor pulled into the parking lot of his daddy's place. Then he just stared at his hands on the steering wheel like maybe something had been written in code there.

A big fly buzzed into the truck and landed on the paper that had held a three-pack of Twinkies. I watched it shining green eyed and almost pretty.

Taylor cleared his throat. "Sometimes you act cranky with me," he said. "It's a lot more embarrassing when there are people around to hear it."

"Oh." I fanned my hand at the fly and it buzzed up into the air then back down again. "I'm sorry," I said.

"Yeah?" Taylor said. He sat quiet a moment. "I really appreciate that, Honey."

I got out of the truck feeling kind of clean inside, good almost, and started for home.

"Wait, Honey," Taylor called.

I looked back as he galloped around the truck and over to where I stood in the late afternoon sun. The sky had clouded up. It might rain soon.

"What is it, Taylor Hiatt?" I said. And I didn't use an ugly voice. I was nice.

He stood in front of me, greasy T-shirt, old blue jeans, big eyes, and all. "Someday I think you really are gonna love me back."

"Taylor Hiatt," I said. I swung around toward home, my hair spinning out as I twirled. I stomped down the sand and rock driveway away from Taylor and the Sinclair green-dinosaur gas station.

"I just want you to know that I'll wait for you to change your mind about me," Taylor called. "I'll wait as long as I have to."

His words, loud in the late afternoon air, caused a rush of confusion. I liked him. I didn't. I liked him. I didn't. I liked him.

"Good-bye, Taylor," I yelled, and took off running.

Chapter 11

IT WASN'T LONG BEFORE ME AND CHRISTMAS were inseparable. It seemed that she needed to hang around. She was always learning new things.

Like it was okay to put your elbows on the table and that families really did eat together here in America. She spent the night at my place and was surprised when Momma came out to the tree house to make sure we had smeared Avon bath lotion all over us so the mosquitoes wouldn't eat us up while we slept. Christmas said she couldn't remember the last time Miriam had tucked her in, that was Maude's job.

But the biggest thing to Christmas was Pop-Pop.

One afternoon we rode our bikes to the diner. I'm not sure why. It was closed and I knew it was closed, but we had spent the entire day working on the tree house and we needed a break.

Christmas guided her bike up to the window and peered in.

I pushed myself over to her with my feet, and, leaning

on my bike on the ledge, looked through the window, too.

I couldn't tell what Christmas was staring at. All I could see were the things I always see. The pictures, the counters and stools and the red booths, and the glassless window that Daddy stands behind so he can put out the orders. Everything was sun and shadow zebra striped because of the blinds.

"I knew we'd be friends as soon as I saw the pictures," Christmas said. Her voice was soft and I wasn't sure if she was talking to me or to what was hanging on the walls. "That's what I told my dad when he called for me to visit."

I glanced back to the large black-and-white posters, then over at Christmas. Her forehead rested on the glass.

"Well," I said. "None of those are mine. They all belong to my momma."

"What I wouldn't give to meet him." Christmas breathed out a big sigh and a circle of steam fogged up the glass by her mouth then disappeared.

"They're nearly all dead," I said.

"Not the Reverend Gaynor T. McKenna."

"No," I said, not at all surprised that Christmas knew about him. Seems just about everyone does. "Pop-Pop sure is alive and well."

"What do you mean, Pop-Pop? That's the Reverend Gaynor T. McKenna, star of the *Five Alive* morning show."

"I know. He's my grandfather."

I thought Christmas might faint. She gasped and clutched at her heart. I mean she really clutched at her heart.

I got off my bike and propped it up against the wall.

"You're lying to me," she said.

I felt a little indignant. "I don't lie," I said. "Not hardly ever."

"It's a sin," Christmas said.

"Well, yeah, I guess. But mostly Momma gets real mad if I lie to her or to Daddy. So I try to stick to the truth. Unless it's to save my hide."

Christmas was torn away from the window now, by my words, and looking at me. "Like when have you lied?"

I thought. "Well, once Willie-Bill stole some of Daddy's vodka and drank it straight out of the bottle just like he'd seen some kids do on TV. I told him not to, but him and Taylor did it anyway. Then I tried it myself. Only took a tiny sip 'cause it tasted so bad."

"You get used to the taste if you drink it long enough," Christmas said. "Easter told me so."

That didn't surprise me none.

"Easter's spent time at Betty Ford's place," Christmas said.

"Who's Betty Ford? A relative of yours?"

Christmas looked at me like I was real dumb. "It's a place for alcoholics."

"Oh," I said. I couldn't think of anything else to say and I was feeling dumb now.

"She nearly died."

"Betty Ford?"

"No, Easter."

"You are kidding me," I said. "I can't believe it."

"Yeah, she's an alcoholic." Christmas said this so matter-of-fact that I wondered if maybe *she* was lying. "So then what happened to Willie-Bill?"

"Uh," I said.

"After he drank the vodka?"

My mind felt numb. "Uh," I said again. "He got really sick."

"Is that the whole story? He got sick?" The way Christmas said it, what happened to Willie-Bill wasn't much of a story, not compared to Easter and all.

"He got real sick," I said. "And Momma wanted to know if I'd drunk any vodka, too. I told her no."

Christmas looked at me like, So? Then she said it. "So?"

"So that's one of the lies I've told. You wanted to know one, so there you have it."

Christmas kind of nodded.

"That's not much of a lie."

"Sorry," I said. Then I laughed a little. I mean, I'm not going to start lying just to tell a good story.

"I lie," Christmas said. "Mostly to Miriam and Easter."

She looked away and back through the plate-glass window that reflected spots of light here and there.

"You are related to a true saint," she whispered. She reached her hand out and touched my shoulder. It was like she couldn't believe I was there. Like maybe she thought I was a ghost or an angel or something.

"Maybe you can meet him sometime," I said.

"You're kidding me?" Something happened right then. Christmas talked to me like she really had feeling. Here we had talked about her sister almost drinking herself to death and about her not having a dad around and about having a mom who really didn't care and Christmas had been kind of ho hum about the whole thing. Now she was out and out excited.

"I mean it," I said. "Pop-Pop comes for dinner every week. You can come, too, and meet him."

"I cannot believe that my life has changed so much and all because we moved here, Honey," Christmas said and she touched my shoulder again. "You really do live in Heaven."

I grinned, and feeling generous, said, "You could even invite Easter and Miriam if you wanted. Maude, too. Momma wouldn't mind." As soon as the words were out though, I thought Momma would mind a whole lot. That's one thing about my mouth. Sometimes I think it has a mind of its own.

"Miriam and Easter?" Christmas was flabbergasted. I could tell by the way her eyes got so big and all.

"Sure, why not?" I moved away from the window. I sat on a red bench that our customers sometimes sit on when there's no room inside. After a moment or two, Christmas came and sat down, too.

"Well, because of my mother," she said.

"What about your mother?"

Christmas lowered her voice and leaned toward me. "She's Miriam Season."

I nodded. "So?"

"So? She's . . . well, she's a movie star . . . with no morals. She's interested in her career. That's it. That's all. She only loves herself."

There was nothing to say to that. I didn't know if Miriam Season loved only herself or everyone. I'd only met her one time.

"But your Pop-Pop," she said, "he loves the world."

"Yeah," I said, knowing it was true and remembering right then how he feels about me, "he does love people."

Christmas sucked in a big breath and squinted at the sky. "What if I don't want them to come?"

I felt a bit of relief at her words. "You don't have to invite them," I said. "I was thinking maybe you'd want to, you know, just 'cause. But, you know, if you're feeling like maybe they wouldn't want to come, or something, then, you know, you could not invite them."

"Mostly I'm feeling like I don't want to invite them at all." Christmas looked at me, her blue eyes kind of sad, like the first night I had seen her at the diner. "I don't think I want them around at all."

And I left it at that.

Chapter 12

THE FOLLOWING SATURDAY, CHRISTMAS CAME
tearing up to the house on her bike.

"Honey," she called from the front porch. "Honey."

"Come on in," I heard Momma say from the kitchen.
"Come visit me in here, Christmas."

I clattered down the stairs from my room. "Hey," I
said.

"Hey." Christmas had our lunch bag in one hand and
a cream-colored card in the other.

"Well, it sounds like it'll be interesting, to say the
least," Momma was saying.

"Not to me," Christmas said.

"What?" I said.

"Miriam's throwing a party tonight. I hate her par-
ties."

"Yeah? Why's that?" I asked.

"She forces me to play the piano, she makes me pass
around hors d'oeuvres, then I'll have to go to bed when
I'm no longer cute and when I'm in the way," she said.

"I didn't know you were that good on the piano."

Christmas nodded. "Yeah, music and me are like this." She held up her hand, her fingers crossed in an "I'm hoping" sign.

Christmas moved close to Momma, snuggling in under her arm. "So this invitation is for you and your husband."

Momma made a grimace at me over the top of Christmas's head. "That's real nice of your mother to think of us."

"You going to the party?" I asked Momma.

She shook her head and her curly hair waved around. "Probably not. Your daddy has a paper to work on and we can't just close up the diner."

Nice save, I thought, and grinned at Momma. "Let's get outta here, Christmas." And we left.

Outside, the weather was perfect, the sky full of puffy, white clouds. There was a little bit of a breeze blowing, just enough to cool you down in sweaty places.

"So what are you gonna do?" I asked Christmas, who gnawed at her already chewed-off nails.

"Go bike riding with you."

"I mean about the party?"

We started out my drive toward the highway, our tires making crunching sounds on the shells.

"Oh, that. I'm not sure. But I have been thinking."

"About what?"

"How to get out of this. I have a plan."

We turned on the highway in the direction of Christmas's place. We'd nailed up some foundation boards in the oak and I wanted to go back and see if they still looked as good as they had. "Tell me what your plan is."

"I was hoping that you'd let me stay with you tonight. Maybe I could even move into your tree house for a day or two."

"What?" I said, my steering getting all wobbly with the surprise.

"Nobody would have to know," Christmas said. She didn't look at me, just stared straight ahead.

"What would Miriam say about that?" I said.

"Who even cares?" Christmas said. And her voice was all mad sounding.

I STAYED WITH CHRISTMAS that entire day, us making ourselves a picnic lunch and later, a picnic dinner. We worked on her tree house awhile, then came back to my home again. I left Christmas late in the evening, almost before the sun had set completely, getting ready to camp in the tree house, with a flashlight so we could communicate after dark.

"I'll be fine alone," she assured me, and I went home.

Momma was waiting for me and Willie-Bill when I came in through the back door and into the kitchen, too late for dinner. And she wasn't wearing a smile. Even her hair looked angry. She probably wouldn't have made a very good guest at any party right at that moment.

"Where have you been?" she said. Her hands were on her hips like maybe she was holding herself down.

I started in fast because I knew I wasn't gonna have a chance if I didn't. "Now wait a minute, Momma."

"No, Honey Marie DeLoach, *you* wait a minute."

I've always been real glad my middle name isn't Comb.

"I just want to tell you something—"

"I just want to tell *you* something," Momma said. And since her voice was lots louder than mine, I let her talk. I didn't have a choice. I'd lost my chance at getting heard tonight.

"Why are you late?"

"Momma, I was getting ready to tell—"

"You know dinnertime is family time. I don't ever want you to be late to dinner. That's the rule and it's always been the rule and it always will be the rule, even after you are married and have children and live five hundred miles away from home."

"I know, Momma, but—"

"Don't but me, young lady. Do you know how worried I was? Where have you been?"

"Me and Christmas—"

"What in the world were you two doing? I swear to my name, between you and Billy . . . I was getting ready to call the sheriff, and you know how long it takes for the police to get out here. I was talking to your daddy about getting up a search party. But there's so few people in this area, and so much land I knew we'd never find either of you. I almost called Pop-Pop." Momma paused to take a breath, so I leaped in to tell my part of the story. I saw Daddy standing in the doorway.

"Me and Christmas were sitting—"

"This better not happen again or I'll restrict you from going outside so long that you'll forget what a breeze feels like. Where's Billy? Wait till I get my hands on him," Momma said. She turned around and stomped from the room. She was so angry she slammed the door on her way out.

It doesn't do any good to argue with Momma. She cuts you off quicker that your heart can beat. I've done my best trying to squeeze words in sideways between what she's saying but it never works. I've even tried cramming my words in between hers. Nothing's successful. The only person I know who can argue her down is Daddy. At least I *think* he could. I'm not so sure 'cause I've never seen them do any real arguing.

I looked over at my father. He's the opposite of Momma. He says hardly anything when he's mad. I felt his eyes boring a hole in me.

"First of all," I said. "I don't know where Willie-Bill is."

Daddy crossed his arms in front of himself. That was not a good sign.

"I didn't mean to be late. We had a picnic lunch. Then we made the rounds. You know, went riding and tree house building. Then we just talked. We ended up here in the yard." My voice dwindled down to nothing.

Daddy lowered his head a little, reminding me of the charging Mormon bull. Only he's not a Mormon. My daddy, I mean.

"We did, Daddy. Right in the back acre part. If yawl had peeked out the window you'da seen our bikes."

"You missed dinner," Daddy said.

"I'm sorry. We were talking. And we ate. And just had a good ol' time together. Christmas sure has been happy since we started being friends."

"Well, I don't know if you noticed your momma, but *she* was very unhappy." Daddy came over to me and hugged me up close, then kissed the top of my head. "Mostly she's worried about Bill."

"Daddy," I said, knowing I could talk now that his voice was softening up a bit. "Daddy, things aren't so great for Christmas. I mean, nobody's hitting her or nothing. But she's sad living over there." Suddenly I felt tired.

Daddy took in a deep breath, then let it out slow. "Honey, if there was one thing I learned when I was a lawyer, it's that you can't save the world. Hustle on up to bed and think of that."

And so I did. I wondered a lot about what Daddy meant by saving the world and I wondered a lot about what Pop-Pop would say about this whole thing. I was glad he'd be over soon.

Then I started thinking about Christmas and how distant she could be. In my thinking of our time together, I remembered her like I was looking through a thick piece of glass. Talking with her was like talking to somebody who doesn't let you all the way in. She was full of secrets. I was sure the secrets somehow involved Miriam Season and Easter, but mostly involved a hurt inside Christmas that seemed to be real deep. To me it was awful sad.

I thought about Daddy again, and his saying I couldn't save the world. I didn't want to save anything at all, truth be told. I only wanted to see my friend happy.

THEY DIDN'T GO TO bed, Momma and Daddy. Instead, the two of them sat up in the living room and waited for my brother to get home.

I crawled to my window. The whole backyard was dark as pitch. The night sky was full of stars and just a thin slice of moon.

Between where me and Christmas were, lightning bugs lit up with their own messages. Was she still awake?

I knelt on the floor, paper, pencil, and flashlight at the ready. I turned on the flashlight, one long shot, then waited for Christmas to return the signal. A shaft of light seemed to burst from the tree house.

I grinned.

"Are you scared out there all alone?" I flashed to her. Only it took a long time. A real long time. We were doing the alphabet deal. You know, one flash for A, two for B, 26 for Z.

"No," she flashed back. "But there are a lot of mos-quitoes."

We talked for a while, not saying much, beaming our signals through the dark.

Crouching near the window I heard Momma and Daddy go to bed, but I didn't hear Willie-Bill come in.

When I was too tired to hold my eyes open any longer, I shot three drawn out beams that meant good night. Christmas answered me the same way. I flashed the light off and on as fast as I could. This meant signing off. I waited for Christmas's answer, then I climbed back into bed.

YELLING WOKE ME UP. At first, the loud voices worked into my dream and three dogs with curly hair shouted at each other. One of the dogs wore an eye patch.

Then I was all the way awake.

"I'm almost fifteen. I know lots of people whose parents leave them alone to do what they want." Willie-Bill was talking funny, his words slurred and loud.

"And those children don't come home drunk," Momma said.

Drunk? I untangled myself from my covers and sat up in bed.

"I'm not drunk. And I'm not a child."

I heard Daddy mumble something, but I couldn't hear what it was.

"Do I have to watch you every second of the day?" Momma's voice trembled. The sound of it made me feel sad.

"You do watch me every second. That's why I see Easter. She lets me be me. She lets me take in a free breath."

"Go to bed. You don't know what you're talking about."

"I sure as hell do," Willie-Bill shouted. "Me and Easter's been talking about it. We been talking about how you don't let me live."

"Uh-oh," I whispered.

"Don't talk to your mother that way," Daddy said.

At the same time Momma said, "I knew that girl was trouble." And it wasn't like Momma hated Easter. It was like she just knew, and was sorry that she knew, the kind of person Easter was.

"Go to bed, Billy," Daddy said. "You need a chance to . . . to rest."

"I'm fine," Willie-Bill said. "I'm fine. My stomach hurts, though."

"Great," Momma said. "You take care of him. I'm worn out. I'm going to sleep."

But knowing my momma and the way she feels about us, she didn't sleep a wink. Especially with all that puking going on.

Willie-Bill threw up for a long time, like they show in all the movies. Only this wasn't funny at all. It was just plain ugly. And it scared the hell outta me.

Chapter 13

I GUESS THERE'S NO NEED SAYING WILLIE-BILL didn't get up with the chickens. In fact, I heard Momma offer him something for breakfast and he made a squeaky kind of noise.

I clattered down the stairs, dressed for church, and ran outside to check on Christmas first thing. She was waiting for me.

"Big trouble at my place," I said.

"Oh no, what?" Christmas still wore her jammies. She was also scratching. There really must have been a lot of mosquitoes.

"Willie-Bill came home drunk from being with Easter."

Christmas didn't say anything at first, just swallowed a couple of times. Then, "Is your mother mad at me?"

" 'Course not," I said. I decided not to mention her being unhappy with me 'cause I was late. "But she's fit to be tied with Willie-Bill. 'Cause of what they did. And this drinking thing sure didn't help."

Christmas blinked a couple of times.

"I gotta go," I said. "Are you 'showing up' for breakfast?"

"I'm scared to now, Honey."

"What do you mean?"

"This thing with Willie-Bill. Maybe Mandy will blame me." Christmas stood there in the middle of my tree house, so nervous I couldn't believe it.

"Nah, that's not Momma. Believe you me, she puts blame where it's due." *That* was the truth. Momma might never let you get a word in edgewise, but she's fair and swift. "Get dressed and pretend to show up in a few minutes. You almost always come for breakfast anyways. It would be weird if you didn't."

"That's true," Christmas said, and she started chewing on her nubby fingernails.

I turned to crawl out the tree house door, but Christmas stopped me.

"Hey, Honey," she said.

"Huh?"

"Remember a long time ago I told you never to let people know what you're scared of?"

I nodded. I could hear a bobwhite calling. The sun was rising crisp and pure, slinging arrows of light in our direction, painting things beyond the tree house golden with color.

"There's something worse than dying to me."

"No way," I said, my voice coming out all breathy and surprised. I took a step toward Christmas. What could be worse than that? Not including not being saved, I mean.

"Not being able to be your friend anymore."

I gasped. "What are you talking about?"

Christmas's voice got shaky, like maybe she was gonna start crying.

"If you weren't my friend I don't know what I'd do."

I practically ran to Christmas and threw my arms around her neck. "I'll always be your friend," I said into her short hair. "No matter what happens I will always be your friend."

Christmas hugged me back hard, almost squeezing the breath outta me.

"Honey." It was Momma, calling out the kitchen window. "Time for breakfast."

"I gotta go," I said. "Hurry on up and change, then give us a few minutes and come eat."

Christmas grinned right in my face. "I'll be there."

Chapter 14

FINALLY, FINALLY, CHRISTMAS WAS GOING TO meet Pop-Pop. It was Monday, more than a week after Miriam's party. Things had settled down at the house some. Pop-Pop was expected at our place any minute. I decided to pedal on over to Christmas's and get her.

I rang the bell once I arrived at The Mansion and waited. Maude, Christmas's nanny, answered the door. It looked to me like she'd been crying, and she didn't do anything except call for Christmas and leave. I stood in the cool foyer.

Christmas didn't come down and didn't come down. Where was she?

I let myself out of the house and stood on the huge porch. The sound of hammering came to me then, soft like a distant woodpecker.

Of course! The tree house.

I ran across the large circular drive, and past the pool and then the garages. Over the grass and toward the hammering I went.

"Christmas," I called when I got close enough to the

tree that I could see the mark Taylor had made with the bumper of his daddy's truck. The memory made me smile. "Christmas."

"Honey?" Christmas peered out through oak leaves.

"You ready to get a move on? Pop-Pop's waiting."

"I am." Christmas climbed down and we started for my home.

On the way Christmas cleared her throat, then said, "Miriam fired Maude. She has three days to get out."

"What?" My voice was all breathy. "What in the world happened?"

Christmas stared at the road ahead. "Miriam's always firing Maude," she said after a long minute. "But today, Maude started packing, then came into my room and said good-bye. She said she wouldn't come back. She said I'm getting old enough that she doesn't need to stay anymore."

"Now what?" I asked.

"I don't know."

"Are you sad about it?"

"What difference does being sad make? I can't do anything about it. And my sadness doesn't change anything. I'm pretty sure she won't come back this time."

Songbirds twittered in the trees next to us and a hot breeze pushed through them making the leaves rustle. I could hear grasshoppers chirping and from far away came the sound of a horn blowing. I kept on pedaling.

"It almost doesn't seem legal," I said. "She's been with you so long."

We rode the rest of the way in silence.

Pop-Pop's truck was parked in front of our place. We jumped off our bikes, letting them clatter to the ground.

"Wait," Christmas said, before we had even made it to the front porch. "How do I look?"

I was surprised. "You're worrying about your looks?"

"If you don't mind."

"I don't," I said. "It's just you've never really cared before."

"True," Christmas said, trying to catch a glimpse of herself in the small window of our front door. "It's just this is your mother's father. And I want her to be proud of me."

"You look just fine. Not that it would matter to Pop-Pop or Momma. He thinks it's a person's heart that's important. So does she."

"Yeah, I know." Christmas ran her fingers through her hair anyway, then with slow steps, began to make her way inside again.

We squeaked the door open.

Sunlight splashed through the west window, lighting the front room all orangey gold, dyeing the cream-colored sofa a matching sun color.

Down the short hall we went, on tiptoe, the voices in the sunroom getting louder.

I could hear Momma plain. Her voice was worried.

"It's that Season girl's lifestyle that bothers me so much," Momma was saying.

I felt my face color.

Christmas put her finger to her lips to keep me from talking.

"Not everyone has the beliefs you do," Pop-Pop said. "Remember that and be forgiving."

"I know that, Poppy," Momma said. "But her mother has no values at all. And it's obvious that it's rubbed off on the child. And Billy, too."

I glanced at Christmas, then leaning close said, "They're talking about Easter."

"And my mother," Christmas whispered back, her face red.

Momma kept going. "Wonder if that girl leads my child astray. Already there are changes in his behavior. Billy has never acted so resentful before."

"He's young, Mandy. He's got to learn for himself. You can't make him believe the things you believe." Pop-Pop's voice was soothing.

Christmas nodded her head at me. "I'm glad I didn't invite Easter and Miriam," she said, the tops of her ears red.

I made myself call out. "Momma," I said. My voice sounded funny to my ears. "We're coming down the hall." I stamped my feet a couple of times. And Christmas and I walked into the sunroom.

Daddy was in his easy chair, but sitting straight up and at attention. Momma stood near one of the windows that line the east wall. She looked uncomfortable. Probably because we had caught her in the midst of gossiping. Pop-Pop was the only one who didn't look like he'd gotten something caught in his craw. He wore what he always wears when he's not preaching: blue jeans, a T-shirt (plain white), and a pair of canvas shoes.

As soon as Christmas stood in the doorway, she let out a gasp. I looked around quick to see what had surprised her so. I cleared my throat to make introductions, but Christmas was over to Pop-Pop before I could even start.

"My brother in Jesus," she said. And her voice came out all feathery.

For a minute I wondered if she was gonna go down on one knee or ask to get baptized.

Pop-Pop reached out and Christmas grabbed his hand tight with both her own. He looked Christmas straight in the eye and his face got all happy looking. He sure does like being recognized. He wants people to know him for good or evil. At least that way, he says, he knows people are hearing The Word.

"It's a pleasure to meet you, too," he said, and I knew he meant it.

Something funny happened to me then. It was like I saw Christmas for what she really was: a lonely, sad little girl.

It was there only a second, my vision: Pop-Pop holding on to my friend, reaching out and putting his free hand on her shoulder. And Christmas hanging on to him for dear life. Then it was gone and things didn't seem so intense. Christmas didn't look so sad and lonely. And Pop-Pop looked like a normal person and not a saver of souls.

"Let's go eat," Momma said, breaking up what was left of the spell. "Country fried chicken."

"And bread," Pop-Pop said. "I can smell it."

"Me, too," said Christmas, and she smiled at me.

By the time dinner was over, Pop-Pop and Christmas were best friends. She practically snuggled into him, sang a beautiful version of "How Great Thou Art" while Momma played the piano for her, and then told everybody how she had been singing since before she was even born.

And prior to his leaving Pop-Pop invited Christmas and her family to come and hear him at the summer revival meeting the very next night.

Chapter 15

THAT EVENING WE SAT OUT IN FRONT OF THE diner. Pop-Pop had gone home and the chauffeur was coming to pick Christmas and her bike up.

"Christmas," I said. "What's going on with Willie-Bill and Easter?"

She shrugged. "I don't know."

"He's acting like a weirdo," I said. "Momma's all bent outta shape with worry. I wish I knew what was going on."

"Maybe you should try talking to him."

I thought for a second. "I don't know if I remember how. It's been so long since we were talking friends, it seems."

"Come on, Honey," Christmas said. A mosquito landed on her arm and she slapped at it. "I know you better than that. You've got guts."

"You think so?" I was surprised at Christmas's compliment.

"Yes, I do. So think about all your brave moments, gather up your nerve and go talk to him."

The distant odor of skunk floated over to us. A breeze puffed up and pushed the smell away, thank goodness.

"I guess I should," I said. "What should I say?"

Christmas shuffled her feet on the ground, leaning a little on her bike. "Tell him you miss him. Tell him you remember times when the two of you used to laugh together."

"I might be able to do that." The idea of it all fit comfortable in my head.

Christmas looked at me, her eyes shiny in the darkness. "Tell him, 'Nothing's more important than family.' Your grandfather said those very words this evening."

"Did he?"

"Maybe you should just say to him . . ." Christmas threw a leg over her bike. "Maybe you should just say to him, 'Let's be friends. Don't go anywhere. Stay here close to me. I love you.' "

"What?"

"I can't wait any longer," she said. "Not for someone to come get me. Maude's leaving." Tears started streaming down her face. Christmas looked at me. The light that marked our driveway out to passersby flickered on and shone in the wetness on her cheeks. "Family is what's important, Honey. I saw that tonight, with you and Pop-Pop and Mandy and your father and brother. Even with how unhappy your mom is with Willie-Bill, love is most important. I've got to get home. I've got to tell Maude good-bye."

And Christmas was off without another word,

pedaling fast and furious down the darkening road, finally disappearing in the twilight.

I found Willie-Bill in his bedroom. "Willie-Bill," I said. "Let's you and me talk."

He was reading a magazine about motorcycles.

His eyes narrowed a little. "Why should we?"

I flopped at the foot of his bed. Starting out with Easter first thing wouldn't work. " 'Member that one time you and me and Taylor decided to walk to Disney World?"

Willie-Bill plumped up his pillows and settled back into them. "What in heck made you think of that?"

I shrugged, then breathed in deep. "I just been thinking about you and me."

"Why's that?" Willie-Bill was looking suspicious again.

I got up and went to stand near his window, so I could look out at the side yard. "I don't know. I been missing you and me together. Like we used to be. Before."

"Before what?"

"Before whatever it was that changed us." I turned around and looked at my brother, all comfortable on his blue bedspread, shoes making sandy-looking marks on the covers, magazine pinched between his fingers.

"We used to have a good ol' time. Before."

"Now don't you go blaming Easter, too," he said.

"I'm not." And I wasn't. The change was long before the Seasons moved here, though I couldn't really point out a day and say, "It happened then."

"You sure?"

"I'm sure."

Willie-Bill tossed his magazine on the floor where he'd piled a whole lot of other stuff, too, like his running shoes and dinner clothes and some things that looked like they didn't make it into a wastebasket. "She's a real nice girl, Easter is," he said, and his voice was as soft as a feather pillow. He wasn't looking at me anymore, but kind of gazing into his hands, like maybe he held a picture of her there.

I sat back down on his bed.

"When I go over to her place, we watch movies together, and we hold hands." Willie-Bill's face turned red at the memory, or maybe because he was sharing. "And she's got herself some nerve."

"I know that's right," I said. You could see just by looking at Easter that was the truth.

"Promise you won't tell?" Willie-Bill said. "Promise on our good times together back in the olden days."

I scooted closer to my brother. "Yeah," I said. "I promise. What is it?"

"One night I heard this tapping at my window and when I got outta bed she was there, like Spider-Man or something."

I looked at his window, closed against the hot night air. "Whatdaya mean?"

Willie-Bill put his head close to mine, his eyes shining. "I mean, she was out there on the roof. She'd come up on one of the columns that hold up the porch."

"You are kidding me."

Willie-Bill shook his head. "I am not. She told me . . ." Willie-Bill stopped with his memories to enjoy them. "She told me she missed me, Honey."

"Time for bed," Daddy shouted upstairs. "We'll be having family prayer in ten minutes."

"And then what happened?"

"I ain't telling you another word." Willie-Bill raised his eyebrows at me like, Don't you wish you knew?

"That was good," I said to myself, later, in the shower. "That was a real good conversation. Except for that one eensy-weensy little place where Easter snuck into his room. The rest was okay." I didn't want that kind of information from Willie-Bill. But I realized I *did* want to be his friend. "And that's gonna happen," I whispered into the spray. The hot water seemed to soothe my worried feelings. "Me and Willie-Bill are gonna be good friends again."

The phone rang right after I climbed outta the shower and was putting on my jammies.

Momma tapped on the bathroom door. "Christmas for you, Honey," she said.

"Coming." I hurried into my room, a towel wrapped like an old-fashioned beehive on my head.

"Hello?"

"She's gone," Christmas said. "She was packing when I got here and she didn't even stop when I chased the taxi down the road. I'm all alone now." And then Christmas was crying.

Chapter 16

I HAVE TO TELL YOU RIGHT HERE AND NOW
that Pop-Pop is one damn good preacher and I mean that
as a compliment. I've been to plenty of revivals, Pop-
Pop's and the competitions', and his are by far the best.
Even if I haven't been saved yet.

The next night I went and waited out on the front
porch for Christmas to pick me up. Her momma was supposed to drive us into Orlando in her Mercedes convert-
ible and I was kinda glad about that. Miriam Season was
a mystery to me still, and Christmas and I had been
friends for what seemed like years even though it had only
been part of one summer. I felt like I had always known
Christmas, since before she was born even, though I don't
know how that's possible.

I sat on the front porch step and waited. Inside I could
hear an argument going on between Momma and Willie-
Bill.

"I said, no," Momma said.

"Why not? Why can't I go over there? Honey gets to

do what she wants." Willie-Bill was pretty angry. I could hear it in his voice.

I breathed in deep and smelled the coming of night, hot and relaxing and promising.

"You cannot go because I said you cannot go," Momma said. There was the sound of a clink of glasses. "And this is not about Honey."

"Daddy, tell Momma I can go."

No answer.

I looked out at the Florida 8 P.M. sky. Even the intense blue of the heavens seemed perfect.

"Just tell me why," Willie-Bill said.

Tree frogs began singing for rain all at once. It was like someone had lifted a baton and started the choir of skinny green things together for this evening song.

"I love the frogs," I said to the sky.

"Because, damn it, I told you no," Momma said.

"You better listen to your momma," Daddy said. "You're starting to get under her skin. You know what happens once she gets riled."

I heard the clink of ice in a glass. Daddy must be sitting in his favorite chair sipping tea. But he sure couldn't be comfortable with that argument going on.

"I told you no because, William Samuel DeLoach, I know that girl is trouble. There will be trouble if you keep on seeing her."

"Hormones and my almost fifteen-year-old son," Daddy said, almost in song himself. The frog chorus seemed a perfect background.

I pulled my knees up to my chin and waited. Dragonflies zipped this way and that, catching mosquitoes, I hoped. From far away I heard a rooster crow. I rubbed my teeth on my knee, making a squeaking sound.

"I'd appreciate it, Joseph, if you'd start supporting me," Momma said to Daddy. "And Billy, I'd appreciate it if you started listening and accepting what I say to you. It's not very often that I don't let you do something you want to do."

"Momma, come on," Willie-Bill said. "There's never been nuthin to do out here, that's why you've never stopped me from it. You've got Honey and me stashed so far away from the real world that it's a wonder I even know what a girl is."

Daddy laughed a small laugh that seemed to echo around in his glass. "Believe me, boy, at your age you could be on a deserted island off the coast here and you'd know what a woman was the moment you saw her. Thanks to hormones."

"Joseph," Momma said and her voice was a caution.

I stood and peered into the house through the screen door.

"I'm walking on down to the diner to meet Christmas," I called.

"All right, Honey," Momma said.

"See," Willie-Bill screeched out. "See what I mean? You'll let Honey do whatever she wants."

I was halfway into the yard by then, so I didn't hear

Momma's answer. But I could hear the growl of her voice and I knew it was dangerous.

I closed my eyes for a moment as I walked down the road that led to the diner.

Along one side of the driveway, trees grew in thick. A bit of cool air seemed to reach out to me from this spot. As I came close to the woods the frogs stopped, waiting for me to pass, then the chorus began again.

Up ahead, coming down the long strip of road that connected my house with Christmas's, I saw the limo. I stopped short, surprised. Then I began to run, sprinting toward the diner so I could meet Christmas there.

Miriam Season is driving the limo, I thought. I made it to the diner just a moment or two before the car did, and stood there.

"Hey, you!"

It was Taylor. I looked over at him. He was cleaning up before the station closed down for the night. He waved a push broom at me.

"Hey," I said.

The limo pulled into the parking lot, crunching the gravel underneath its tires.

"Where you going?" Taylor called out, and he took a few steps toward me, dragging the broom behind himself.

"To see Pop-Pop," I said, and ran to the door of the car that swung open as I got to it.

"Honey," Christmas yelled from the backseat. She

bounced up and down. "We're going to see your grandfather."

I grinned at her. Then I climbed in and sat down on the dark leather seat. Christmas was the only one in the car, except the chauffeur.

"I'll be happy to help you in from now on," the chauffeur said, looking at me.

"That's okay." I slammed the door shut, closing out the sounds of singing frogs, then waved as we coasted past Taylor. I wasn't sure if he could see me, though. The windows were just too black.

Chapter 17

"WHERE'S YOUR MOMMA, CHRISTMAS?" I ASKED, when I'd settled down from waving at Taylor, then inspected the whole of where we sat.

"She couldn't come," Christmas said.

"I thought she promised she'd drive."

I felt a little disappointed. Would I ever get to know the famous Miriam Season?

"Too bad for her own fat self," Christmas said, using one of the things I sometimes said. "I'm glad she decided not to."

"No, you're not," I said, 'cause I could see plain as the sunlight can be seen that Christmas *did* mind.

"She doesn't have time for me," Christmas said. "And I don't plan on wasting any time worrying about her either."

"Fine by me," I said.

And so we talked of everything there was to talk about except Miriam Season. I told her of my chat with Willie-Bill. We ate from the little fridge that was stocked with mostly champagne and watched cartoons on the television.

Miles went by so quick that I was surprised when we were on the outskirts of Orlando. And in only a few more minutes we pulled up to the tent revival that already swarmed with people, like the ants out back of my house sometimes do.

"People love my Pop-Pop," I said. And I grinned big.

"We'll be out when it's over," Christmas said to the driver. She turned to me. "I got a surprise for you."

"What?"

Christmas's eyes sparkled and I was glad 'cause it didn't seem she was sad about Miriam or Maude anymore. "You'll see. Let's get going."

Christmas and I fell into the lines of people that moved forward into a tent that had no sides, only a top and a front where Pop-Pop would make his entrance. Wooden benches lined the grassy area that had been strewn with straw. Huge speakers were set up all over the grounds area so everyone would be able to hear, right up close and in the next town, too.

Christmas grabbed at my arm. "Honey," she said. "Honey."

That's all she said, but I knew what she meant because I could feel the beginnings of excitement starting to push into me from the very air. It seemed to roll in on us like waves at the beach.

We found a place to sit, not too close to the front, but near an aisle, and there we waited. The hum of people grew heavier. Mosquitoes buzzed near. And then the lights began to dim and the music made a swelling sound reminding me of the ocean.

"Here he comes," I said. "Here comes Pop-Pop."

"Yes, here he comes," Christmas said, and she was on her feet in a second, before anyone else.

Pop-Pop stepped out a moment later, his arms raised, his hair shining white in the lights that came up bright and bore down on him. The audience rose to their feet and the hum became a noise that thundered in my chest and even echoed in my throat. If I had screamed I don't think I could have heard myself. Christmas leaped to stand on her bench, and I stepped out into the aisle so I could see my grandfather.

Pop-Pop settled the crowd with a raise of his arms. He called for the governor of Florida to give the opening prayer, then moved back from the bright lights while the chorister led the group of us in three songs, all melded together into one. For some reason, right at the beginning of our singing, I remembered the frogs' song back home, but then I forgot it almost as quick.

"Brothers and Sisters," Pop-Pop called into the microphone after the singing was done. "Brothers and Sisters, can you believe the feeling of hearts together as one? Imagine the amount of power under this tent at this very moment. Imagine what good we can do."

The audience cheered, and so did Christmas. And so did I. The feeling sure enough was a powerful one.

And then Pop-Pop started his preaching. He walked

back and forth on the wooden platform, waving his arms. He talked about Jesus in Gethsamane, bearing the burdens of sin because of people like us. He showed slides from when he went to Israel. He talked about power and faith and what the two could do together. He talked about the love of God and of Christ. He had people laughing and crying, cheering and muttering. I have to admit, it was one damn good performance.

Then all of a sudden Christmas jumped off her chair and ran to the front of the tent.

"What are you doing?" I meant to shout out, but all I said was, "What?"

Christmas turned and waved and tore up toward Pop-Pop.

I saw when he saw her, 'cause he smiled, but he didn't slow his speaking down none. Christmas stood still looking up at him. After a moment he said to the audience, "I've a visitor. Would you mind if'n I take a moment to talk to her?"

The crowd called that it would be fine.

Pop-Pop bent over to Christmas. People stood to take a break, stretching this way and that.

Sweat ran down my face. It was hot out here.

Pop-Pop motioned to two security guards, who lifted Christmas up onto the stage beside him.

"We have an unexpected surprise," Pop-Pop said. "This here young lady has come prepared to sing for us tonight."

"What?" I said again. My mouth dropped open and with my shoulder I wiped at a little sweat.

Christmas was talking to the lady at the piano and then the members of the rest of the band, who sat back a bit on the stage.

"She wants to remain unnamed so her service will go just as that. A service. I think you'll all be thankful she came tonight."

Pop-Pop adjusted the microphone for Christmas, who leaned toward it and said, "This song . . ." The words boomed out and Christmas leaned away and looked embarrassed. A few of the congregation laughed. "This song is for my good friend in Heaven. The best friend anyone could have. Honey, it's for you."

My breath stopped hot in my throat and for a moment I couldn't even breathe. After a second I managed an "Oh." I felt my face turn red. In case she could see me, I raised my hand, to let her know I had heard.

Christmas turned and nodded at the piano lady, who struck a few chords. The song was one I'd heard Momma sing before. At least the tune was. It was called "Danny Boy" and when Momma sang it, it was pretty enough. But when Christmas sang it, it was like chocolate almost. That chocolate at Willie Wonka's place that ran thick and rich and perfectly creamy down the river in the factory with the Oompa-Loompas.

Christmas had changed the words and when she sang, she sang about being alone all her life even though people surrounded her. And how sad and tired things had become for her. But then she found friends in Heaven and now she felt like she just might make it, even though things were so sad at home.

By the time Christmas was through singing, people all around me were crying. One man, four seats over, had his mouth covered as he sobbed. I swallowed at a lump in my throat and blinked to keep the tears from coming out. But mostly I smiled 'cause I knew Christmas was singing about me and my family.

"Thank you, Reverend," Christmas said when she was done. She stepped back from the microphone and the crowd roared its approval of her. "And thank you, too." Christmas waved her arms out to us all, then jumped down from the stage, landing in the straw. She ran down the aisle, people applauding and reaching for her till she was right near me.

I threw my arms around her neck. "I can't even believe you could do something so great," I said.

"That sure was scary," she said. "Exciting, too."

"Now what did you think of that?" Pop-Pop said, and the crowd went wild again, then people started wiping their eyes and the man four down from me reached over to pat Christmas on the back. I hoped to heaven his hand was dry after all the tears he'd been crying.

Nearing the end of the program Pop-Pop gave the altar call, signaling people to come forward to where he stood. "Have you confessed your sins before God and man?" Pop-Pop called. "Have you come forward and been spiritually born again? Have you been saved?"

I looked over quick at Christmas.

"Come forward," Pop-Pop called out loud and clear. "Come forward and confess your sins and be born again."

People started pouring into the aisle, making their way to Pop-Pop.

"I'm going up," Christmas said. "Come with me, Honey."

Streams of people filed past us, going to where Pop-Pop was praising with each and every one of them. There was going to be a long wait at the pulpit. I knew this from experience. But it wasn't the wait that bothered me. It was the lack of feeling.

"I better not," I said. "You go alone, Christmas."

"I don't want to go alone," she said. "I'm too shy."

I raised my eyebrows.

Christmas laughed. "I am. You don't have to confess." She grabbed my hand. "Just for support, Honey. Come on up for support."

Again, I hesitated.

"I need my friend going up with me," Christmas said. "I don't want to go alone."

I stood and nodded. "I'll go forward with you."

"You're a true friend, Honey DeLoach," Christmas said, coming close to my ear and whispering.

I squeezed her hand. "I sure am glad that you came to Heaven."

We moved forward slow in the crowd, clutching at each other. I'll admit I was hanging on for dear life and this was why: I had never felt such happiness as I did right then. Christmas was my friend. And I knew that was the way it was gonna be until the day one of us died.

It took nearly thirty-five minutes to get up to Pop-Pop. My legs ached by the time we finally got to the front of the tent. The choir had been singing lots of familiar songs, though none compared in beauty to what Christmas had sung. We heard things about the cross Jesus had died on and what a friend He is to us and what scoundrels we are for being the way we are when He is the way He is. All and all I didn't feel much guilt until I was looking Pop-Pop right in the old eyeball.

"Honey," he said. "You've finally come forward." Pop-Pop was still standing on the stage, but he leaped in the crowd where Christmas and I were and grabbed ahold of me in a tight hug. The crowd went wild. Flash bulbs lit things up around us.

"No, Pop-Pop," I said, my voice all muffled in his white shirt. "Not me. I'm not being saved tonight."

Pop-Pop didn't miss a beat or nothing. He hugged me up close and I squeezed him hard back. "I love you, Honey, darling," he said.

Pop-Pop turned me a-loose and swung to face Christmas. Tears were already streaming down her face.

"It's me, Reverend," she said.

Pop-Pop opened his arms wide to Christmas, who threw herself into my grandfather so hard, I wondered for a moment if he might not topple right over. "Praise," she hollered out. Christmas looked up into Pop-Pop's eyes.

"My sweet child," Pop-Pop said. "Have you asked forgiveness of your sins from the One who can forgive?"

"Yes, sir," Christmas said. The bright light hanging high in the tent sparkled on her tears.

"Have you opened the door of your heart to let our Lord and Savior in?"

"Yes, sir."

"Then you are saved," Pop-Pop said.

"Praise to the Host of Heaven," Christmas shouted.

And in that one meeting, Christmas did what I couldn't do in a lifetime.

Chapter 18

EVEN THOUGH I DIDN'T GET SAVED, I STILL felt happy for Christmas. All the way home it was like I rode in a bubble of wonderful feelings. I kept saying a prayer to Heavenly Father about this joy that rolled inside me like a wave spinning toward the shore. It didn't seem like anything would ever change it.

But I was wrong. I could see there was trouble at home before the limo had even pulled up to my place to drop me off.

"Look," Christmas said. "All the lights are on."

I stared off the short distance to my house and my heart started pounding. It was after one in the morning. Momma had known we would be late. Why was every light in the place on?

"Your mother sure is nice to wait up for you like this," Christmas said.

"Yeah," I said. My mouth was dry.

"Nobody'll even know when I walk in."

The limo turned the corner slow into my driveway. Worry pounded at me, making me feel I could run faster than we were being driven. I knew the lights weren't on for me. I leaped out of the car near the front door before we had even come to a complete halt.

"See ya tomorrow, Christmas," I said. "Thank you for that song. I'll remember it forever." Goose bumps ran up and down my arms from fear, but I wanted Christmas to know what tonight had meant.

She peered out the door at me. "I had such a good time," she said. "I love your Pop-Pop. I wish he was mine."

Momma came to the door then. She was only a dark shape because of the way the lights broke all around her. Her shadow stretched out long and bumped its way down the stairs, ending with her head in the front yard.

"And your parents, too," Christmas said. "Somehow, Honey, you made out with it all."

I wanted to answer Christmas, though I wasn't quite sure what to say. So instead, I waved. "See you tomorrow at your tree house," I said, and walked toward Momma.

The limo door closed, making a good connecting sound, and Christmas and her chauffeur drove away.

Momma hadn't moved.

"What is it?" I asked, stepping on her shadow to make it to the porch. "What's wrong, Momma?"

"Your brother is gone."

"Gone?" I felt all the blood drain from my face. It felt like it ended up in my fingertips.

Momma pushed open the screen door for me. "I thought you were him when I heard the car."

"He drove away?" I couldn't believe that. It wasn't that Willie-Bill didn't know how to drive. He did. But the only thing he had ever driven was our tractor.

"No, he took his bike."

I came up to Momma and gave her a hug. I'm getting on to as tall as she is, almost to her ear. I smelled her hair when she hugged me back, clean and almondy smelling. It was soft against my face.

"Where did he go?"

Momma shrugged. "Someplace with Miriam Season's daughter."

"With Easter?"

Momma nodded, but she didn't answer. And I knew that meant trouble. Momma usually has plenty to say, unless she's really angry.

"It'll be all right," I said.

Momma nodded again and worked at her jaw until she got it unloosed. "That girl is trouble," she said at last. "Big trouble. Just like her mother."

I held my breath waiting for Momma to say that Christmas Season was bad blood, too.

"I been telling your daddy and I'll tell you, too, Honey. Those two are trouble with a capital *T*. I only hope that your brother hasn't gone and stirred himself up a nest of something he can't handle." For some reason the thought of the big ant bed out back came to mind. Momma sighed a bit and then turned to look at me. "Go on up to bed."

"Okay, Momma," I said. I leaned over and kissed her.

Momma just kept on staring at the road, waiting on my brother.

I went into the house. Was Willie-Bill stirring up a nest of problems by being with Easter? Was I by being with Christmas? Momma hadn't mentioned Christmas, but maybe that was because she knew how much I wanted a girlfriend.

I undressed and climbed into bed, pulling up only a sheet to cover me. It was too hot for anything else and the air conditioner wasn't on. I heard Daddy come in and knew he was alone. Out my window, past where the curtains waved darker than the night sky, lightning flashed. A storm was coming, which meant the air would only get hotter than it was right now until the clouds broke apart and the rain cooled everything.

Momma's words kept coming back to me. A nest of trouble replayed in my mind until when I finally did go to sleep, I dreamed about the ant bed and that I was stirring and stirring around in it with a big ol' stick, while red ants crawled over me thick, singing tent-meeting songs.

Chapter **19**

WILLIE-BILL CAME HOME AFTER BREAKFAST with Taylor in tow. We had just eaten and I was cleaning off the table, stacking the dishes in the dishwasher.

Momma was furious, I could tell by her quietness. Daddy was pretty mad, too.

"Where've you been?" Momma's voice was harder than the whetstone knife sharpener Daddy uses at the diner.

"At Taylor's place," Willie-Bill said, his eyes darting this way and that, a sure sign he's lying. Taylor looked at the floor. He didn't even give me a passing glance.

"William Samuel DeLoach." Momma's voice was a sad sounding noise.

"I gotta go," Taylor said, under his breath.

"No you don't," Willie-Bill said, his eyes still darting. He made a grab at Taylor, but missed.

Taylor moved to get past me, brushing close. He didn't say a word, but let himself out the back door, closing the screen soft behind him.

"Well that was most unusual," I said. I started to say more, but then I looked around at everyone. Momma was right. The DeLoach nest had definitely been stirred up by the one and only Willie-Bill DeLoach. The stick he was carrying was an awful big one. The lie hadn't helped none.

"Sit down," Daddy said, setting aside the newspaper.

Willie-Bill edged toward his seat, trying to keep one eye on Momma and one on Daddy. This is not an easy thing to do, because whenever anyone is in terrible trouble at my house, our parents always attack from different sides of the room. If it happened to Willie-Bill more often, his getting in trouble I mean, he'd probably have to get glasses on account he'd develop split eye disease.

"How could you?" Momma began.

Willie-Bill sat down, catching the chair with only half his butt.

"Sneaking away was one thing," Momma said. "But running on over where I specifically told you not to, that was even worse."

"Momma, I—" Willie-Bill said.

"Don't you even dare to lie to me again," Momma said.

Daddy didn't say anything, just sat there giving Willie-Bill a terrible stare of the old evil eye.

"But, I—" Willie-Bill said.

"But, I nothing," Momma said. "You left our house without permission and you went with Easter Season. You try to cover it up with a lie about being with Taylor. And dragging that poor boy over here, why, he was the last nail in your coffin."

"I didn't *drag*—" Willie-Bill said.

"Don't you dare get literal with me," Momma said, and her voice went up a little at the end.

If things hadn't been so bad already I might have come to Willie-Bill's defense. For sure no one could drag Taylor anywhere. Unless, of course, that person had a tow truck.

"Son," Daddy said. "You're up the creek without a paddle. Coming clean might save your hide."

"But, Daddy—" Willie-Bill said.

"That's enough," Momma said. "I know where you were and who you were with because I called Miriam Season and she told me. You are in more trouble than you have ever been in your whole life. And I'm just talking about what you have to face here at home. Let me assure you that Easter will cause you plenty of trouble as well. Now go to your room."

"But can't I even—" Willie-Bill asked.

Momma stood up then. "I said go."

Willie-Bill went.

Momma sat down with a thump. She bowed her head, resting it in both hands. "My baby," she said. And sadness crept up into my throat hearing her sound that way.

"You did fine, Mandy," Daddy said. "Just fine."

My parents had forgotten I was there. I stood without

moving, almost without breathing. "Momma," I said, after a moment.

My mother looked at me, and for the first time ever I saw that she was getting old. There were little lines near her eyes, and her forehead had creases in it. Why hadn't I ever noticed it before? "Momma, he really does like Easter a lot. He told me he likes her a lot."

Momma looked at me like she couldn't believe what was coming out of my mouth, then she started to cry, and Daddy reached over for her. It broke my heart to see it.

"Mandy, it'll be okay," Daddy said, and he rubbed at her back, then smoothed his hand down her hair like he was trying to tame the loose curls.

"This will be trouble," Momma said. "I feel it inside. I know it." Her voice was all muffled sounding because she still had her head down.

"Run on outta here, Honey," Daddy said.

I nodded. "Yes, sir." I walked out real slowlike, trying to make sense of all the feelings swirling in my head.

I went upstairs to Willie-Bill's room. I tried to get it out of Willie-Bill, what he had done, I mean, but for sure he wasn't talking. So I did the next best thing. I visited Taylor.

I found him hosing down the carport area of the Sinclair green-dinosaur gas station. There was grease smeared next to his nose. I thought he would squirt me right in the face he was so surprised to see me.

"Honey," he said, and ran the hose on both his own

legs, wetting himself from the knees down. He jerked the hose and the water sailed in a silver arc into the air, almost like it was some kind of wild thing that Taylor tried to tame.

"I come to talk to you about Willie-Bill," I said. "You got time?"

Taylor trotted over to me, still holding the hose. Water splashed on the pavement that looked greasy, like someone had rubbed Crisco over it. It pooled in big bead shapes.

"Sure, Honey," Taylor said, then the hose jerked him to a halt. Water shot up into the air again. Taylor looked down in surprise, then went back into the station and turned the spigot off. He came back, wiping his hands on his half-wet jeans. "I got all the time in the world for you. But we'll have to stay here at the station in case somebody comes by for gas."

"Won't nobody be coming, Taylor," I said, rolling my eyes. "We don't ever get anybody here weekday afternoons. You know that."

Taylor nodded. "Yeah, but my daddy done asked me to stay, so I'm gonna stay. Wanna sit inside?"

I could see two plastic-backed chairs near the glass wall inside the station. They looked grubby.

"Nah," I said, shaking my head. "Let's sit on the sidewalk over at the diner."

Taylor eyed the gas station.

"We'll still be able to see everything, and we're only forty seconds away," I said. "And that's if we walk slow."

Taylor hesitated a moment more, then came up close. "All right, Honey. I'll go over with you." His breath smelled like Fritos corn chips, and it so early in the morning.

Out front of the diner, Momma had set up three rod iron tables with chairs, so when the diner was full, people would still have a place to eat. I led Taylor there. We sat down.

"So what's going on with my brother, Taylor?" I asked, straight up. "He got himself into some trouble for not coming home last night. You know, though, what with him dragging you over this morning."

Taylor leaned toward me. His eyes were blue. So blue they reminded me of ice. I don't mean that they were hard and cold looking. I mean they were blue.

He smiled. A soft smile that almost wasn't there. One I was surprised to find almost attractive. Except for that mark of grease he had on his face.

"You've come over here to tell me about the whole thing," I said.

Taylor's smile grew a little bigger and he leaned closer.

I backed up, my instincts taking over.

"Honey," Taylor said, the smile real big now. "You know I can't tell you nothing about your brother."

"Yes, you can," I said, using my sweetest voice.

Taylor cocked his head a little and adjusted his glasses. "You trying to melt my heart?" he asked.

"Would it make you answer any of what's going on with Willie-Bill if I were?"

Taylor put his finger into a hole in the patterned table-top.

"You're gonna get that stuck," I said.

He pulled at his finger. It turned white as he tried to get it out, but it did come out.

"Taylor," I said, "I want you to tell me what's happening with my brother. A little sister has got to watch out for an older sibling at times."

He leaned back in his chair and tipped a bit. "Honey," he said. "You know I'd tell you just about anything."

"Go ahead then." I settled myself to hear the story. The sun seemed to boil the air around us.

"But I won't be telling you this."

"My momma is about to have an infarction, Taylor. You want my momma to have an infarction?"

Taylor stared at me until I began to feel uncomfortable. Then he shook his head. " 'Course not. I like your momma better'n I like my own."

"You gotta forgive her for leaving sometime," I said.

Taylor glared at me and pinched his mouth shut. I could see we weren't gonna talk about that. We never talk about that.

"Now tell me everything about Willie-Bill," I said, leaning on the table. "You could save a woman's life."

"I'm not telling you nothing," Taylor said. He slid his chair back and it made a painful screeching sound.

Taylor no longer seemed nice. In fact, he seemed infuriating as he always is, probably since the day he was born. Or maybe even before that, if it's possible.

"Then why did you tell me you'd come over here to my place and talk to me?" My voice wasn't sounding too nice.

He stood up. "Just so's I *could* talk to you, Honey. You hardly ever talk to me anymore and I thought I might try . . ."

"Well, you're a devil of deceit," I said, and stood also.

Taylor turned without a word and started back to the gas station. He'd probably stay there the day because his daddy asked him to. Just like I would if Momma or Daddy asked me to. And never utter a complaint like Willie-Bill does even in his sleep, I thought.

He was halfway there when he spun around. "Honey," he said. "Do you think you'll ever like me for who I am?"

"You mean, a gas station attendant?"

"No, I mean Taylor Hiatt. The guy who lives next door."

"I like you for that reason, Taylor," I said. "Especially at a distance."

"Willie-Bill has found someone to love. And she loves him back," Taylor said. "I'll never stop feeling this way about you, Honey. Never." His voice was loud now and his words embarrassed me. I sure was glad that there were only nine people living in Heaven and that only two of us heard this declaration.

The sun made me squint. "Don't wait for me, Taylor. In the real world there's a lot more than nine people. You'll find that out and probably stop liking me." I crossed my fingers for this luck.

He threw his arms up in the air. "I said never. My love is like an eternal flame."

I rolled my eyes to the top of my head, hoping that from that distance Taylor could see what I was doing. "Hell is an eternal flame, too," I said.

Taylor was over to the gas station by now. He bent over for the hose and turned it on full blast, then aimed it at me. The spray of water didn't even come close.

"Well, fine then," I said. "You don't have to get ugly about it." I turned my own self around and started for home, all the while expecting a blast of cold water to somehow hit me in the back.

Chapter 20

THAT AFTERNOON CHRISTMAS CAME OVER after the three o'clock rain shower and we went bike riding. Our plans were to spend a little time at her place, hammering and sawing and trying to get up another side on the tree house.

"That Pop-Pop of yours is wonderful," she said. "I can see where your mother gets her goodness from."

The air was sweet smelling, the ground damp. Everything seemed fresh because of the rain. I love this time of summer, when the day seems new because of a rain. Pop-Pop would call it a cleansing of the earth. It's like this to me every afternoon. Fresh, I mean.

Christmas started talking. It was like she could read my mind. "Some places I've lived," she said, "it's cold after a rain. Some places I've lived, it never rains."

"Really?" I said. "It always rains here. You know that now. And in the winter it can get cold. But I've never seen snow."

"We lived in Idaho. It snowed a lot there."

"Oh yeah?" I said. "I've only lived in Florida and mostly here in Heaven."

I watched the ground as we rolled along. It had a fresh-washed look. Water stood in the ditch beside the road. A dragonfly balanced, shiny and green, on a tall piece of grass that rose from the ditch and bent toward us.

"I've been thinking about something Pop-Pop said last night at the revival."

"What's that?" I said. All I could remember was Christmas's song and my wonderful feeling and that I hadn't gotten saved. Again.

"Well, he talked about Jesus loving everyone."

"Yeah."

We pedaled slow to her house. Sometimes I biked backward, the pedals swirling and whirring but not taking me anywhere.

"And I'm wondering something," Christmas said. "Think of that cow. The one I rode."

"I'm thinking." Who could forget? I wanted to say, but I didn't.

"That cow has never hurt anyone," Christmas said. "She didn't even try to hurt the flies buzzing all around her. She just wagged her tail at them. Like she was happy or something."

"I don't think she was happy," I said. I mean, who could be happy with all those flies buzzing around her face and body? Ger-oss.

"But she didn't try and hurt anything," Christmas said. "That's my point."

I nodded a little because I couldn't help thinking if I had been that cow I would have stood right up on my back hooves and found me a stick to smash flies with. "But that ol' bull tried to get the both of us."

"He was protecting his own. It's okay to take care of your own. Why, your mother's doing it right now with your brother."

"That's the truth," I said. I'm pretty sure Momma could out-mean a bull, especially if it came to her kids. "You know they went off together again last night. And Willie-Bill didn't come home till breakfast."

"Oh no." Christmas squeezed her eyes shut for a second, then opened them again. "Does your mother hate me?"

"No way," I said. I drove over a bumpy part of the road and my voice shook. "Momma thinks you are wonderful."

Christmas was quiet.

"Go on back to what you were saying," I said.

"This all kind of works in," Christmas said. "People are completely different. They're always doing weird things. Trying to hurt others. Not being nice."

"And," I said, drawing out the word 'cause I couldn't really see what she was getting at.

"Honey, you are a rare breed. You are from the loins of the Reverend Gaynor T. McKenna. I saw it at your house and then at the tent meeting that that's what sets you apart. You and your whole family are different because of that one man."

"I hate the word loins," I said.

Christmas wrinkled her nose. "But you know what I mean?"

"I guess," I said. "I don't think we're that great and for sure Willie-Bill isn't happy right now." I thought about Willie-Bill arguing with Momma all the time.

"That's true." Christmas seemed to consider our imperfections. "But at my place people are always trying to hurt each other."

"Trying to?"

"Like Miriam and my father getting a divorce. That was terrible. Or Easter bugging the hell out of Miriam. Or Miriam firing Maude. Or Miriam moving us all the way out here in the middle of nowhere because she thought there'd be no guys for Easter to hang out with."

"That's why yawl came here?" I asked. "Because of Easter?"

"Easter's the reason we run everywhere, Honey. Miriam knew there were two guys here, but your brother is three years younger than my sister. My mother thought Easter would leave him alone."

"What's Easter gonna do to him? To Willie-Bill?" Christmas's family suddenly seemed strange and frightening to me.

"She'll make him fall in love with her. But Miriam thinks Easter's too young for love. That's why we keep

moving. To keep Easter safe. And to avoid my dad."
Christmas stopped walking and looked at me. "I really
do miss my dad, Honey," she said.

And looking at her face, seeing all her sadness right
there, plain as the day, I believed her.

Chapter
21

WELL, WILLIE-BILL WAS IN SERIOUS TROUBLE. Momma put him on restriction, meaning he couldn't leave the yard, use the phone, or go anywhere excepting down to the diner to work.

I thought Willie-Bill had been a terrible complainer before all that, but I was completely wrong. Now it seemed every word outta his mouth was this bad thing about Heaven or that bad thing about Momma and Daddy. He was driving me crazy all over again.

Momma tried reasoning with him but that didn't help none.

"I'm worried about him," I heard Momma tell Daddy more than once when we were at the diner. It had been a whole four days that my brother had been on restriction and all he did was stare out the window like his life was over. I can tell you right here and now that Momma never seemed too worried when she put me on restrictions.

"He's gonna live through this, Mandy," Daddy said. He was preparing vegetables and other food items for the upcoming weekend. "I had punishments much worse than what you've sentenced him to and look at me now." Daddy held his arms out wide and Momma looked at him. "I'm fine."

"Sentenced?" she asked.

"Just clever phrasing," Daddy said.

But Momma didn't smile. "Did your mother ever forbid you to see a girl?"

"Well," Daddy said, drawing the word out long.

"Then how can you know what our son is going through at this very moment?"

I shook my head. Daddy should know better than to step between Momma and her discipline.

"I was trying to make you a little happier," Daddy said, and then he set his big old knife to work, chop, chop, chopping at the ham.

Momma rushed over to Daddy. "I'm sorry," she said, and wrapped her arms around him.

I turned away then, because I knew they were gonna kiss and I think people all over the world need privacy when they do that. Especially those couples on TV. I tell you, I get nearly throw-up sick watching people do that kissy-spit thing.

Willie-Bill was still mooning out the window. With his face, I mean. He practically pressed against the glass. If I had been on the outside looking in, and if I had been starving to death, and if I had seen Willie-Bill staring out the window, I'd have hightailed it past our diner and couldn't nothing of stopped me.

"Get away from the window," I said to Willie-Bill. "You're gonna kill business."

He ignored me.

"Get your sorry ol' behind up and moving around," I said. "You should be sweeping out the place."

Willie-Bill turned slow eyes on me. I don't know if you've ever seen slow eyes, but I did then. "Leave me the hell alone," he said.

I stomped back into the room where we keep all our cleaning supplies and grabbed the broom. I marched back to my brother and presented this gift to him.

"Lookit here," I said. "I'm near about done with my chores and you haven't even begun. I'll tell you right here and now, Mr. Willie-Bill Harold DeLoach, that I am not gonna do your work for you. I always end up doing your work when you putter around and I'm about sick of it."

Willie-Bill looked at the broom. "You can lead a guy to a broom," he said, "but you can't make him sweep."

"What?" I asked.

"I'm not doing nothing, Honey. Nothing."

"You never do anything," I said. "You never help out. You're always moaning and groaning."

"Who are you?" Willie-Bill asked, and his eyes all of a sudden changed from slow, runny-looking things to real mean. "Who are you to tell me anything, Miss Perfect?"

"If I'm Miss Perfect I think I have a right to say what you should do," I said.

Willie-Bill cursed under his breath then. It was one of those words that neither of us is allowed to say.

My eyes got big. "Don't you say that to me." I felt like giving Willie-Bill a great big pinch right on the arm. But I didn't have a chance. It was at that very moment that the long, shiny limo drove up to the diner, crunching its way over the shelly sand of the parking lot.

"Christmas," I said, and at the same time Willie-Bill said, "Easter." It sounded like we were preparing for the holidays.

The driver's door swung open and out came Easter. I waited, but no one else left the car. Darn, I thought. Christmas isn't with her. I felt disappointed for a moment, but a moment was all I had.

Easter walked over to the window where Willie-Bill had frozen into an awkward position. I swear, if I ever fall in love, I will avoid any awkward body positions. They look ridiculous. I'm not kidding. Willie-Bill looked like he had been stopped right when he was getting ready to take a bite from an ice-cream cone. His head was bent low, but his face was forward. His mouth was open. One hand was halfway toward the pane and his back was hunched over.

I heard footsteps and knew Momma was running in from the back room, but I couldn't turn away from what was happening in front of me.

Easter placed her hand on the glass, spreading her fingers wide.

Willie-Bill didn't say anything but let out a little grunt as he moved his own hand onto the glass to match up with Easter's.

"William," Momma said.

Easter's mouth started moving, and for a minute I thought she might kiss the pane that separated the two of them. "I love you," her mouth seemed to say, then she rested her forehead on the window.

Willie-Bill did the same thing with his forehead.

"Oh, Momma," Willie-Bill said. "Help me. Won't somebody help me." But I don't think he was talking to our momma right then.

Easter said some other things. I wasn't exactly sure because I'm not that great of a lip reader, but it appeared to be, "Billy, common do roun fan lettuce et buried." Then I missed some of what she was saying, but the last line was, "I can get a tattoo black as evil on my throat." I might be wrong about that, but I don't think so.

Easter backed away and motioned with one dark nail for Willie-Bill. For a minute I thought he might try to crawl through that plate of glass. But, with his mouth hanging open, Willie-Bill backed out of the booth.

Momma waited for him.

"What are you thinking about doing?" she said, low. The sound of her voice made the hair on my arms stand up.

Willie-Bill cowered back a moment, then pulled himself up straight. He was a good two inches taller than Momma when he did that. I'd never realized he was growing up so big. "Momma," he said.

"Don't Momma me," Momma said.

"I'm going," Willie-Bill said.

"She's getting a tattoo," I said.

"You will stay put," Momma said.

"You can't make me," Willie-Bill said.

"A black heart on her throat," I said.

"What has gotten into you?"

"I'm just saying, Momma, I have my freedom. We live in America."

"I wonder, does she know how many times they'll poke her with a needle? I wonder just how big a heart she wants?"

"I forbid you to go."

"There ain't no law in all of Florida that says I have to do what you say."

"Don't talk like that to your mother." Daddy had worked his way into our circle. He was holding a metal spatula.

"Yawl don't own me," Willie-Bill shouted.

"I do," Momma said, and she was shouting, too. "And I'm concerned for your safety. That girl is trouble." Momma jabbed toward the outside with a napkin she held in her hand.

A tap-tapping sound came from the window. The four of us looked around. Easter still stood outside. A small smile played at her lips.

Willie-Bill broke away from us then and ran. I don't know if he thought Momma and Daddy would chase him or what, but I coulda told him, no they wouldn't.

The door clanged with the sound of the bell and Easter whooped and hopped over to Willie-Bill.

"Like her name," I said. "Hopping like she's some kind of rabbit."

Easter slung her arms around Willie-Bill's neck and he squeezed her to him.

Momma opened the door and the bell clanged again.

"Bill," Momma said. "Stay here. Please."

I don't know what it was about Momma's voice that got to me, but a streak of fear half a mile wide pierced me to my very soul. I came up beside her.

"Billy," I said. "Listen to Momma." My lips were having a hard time moving I felt so scared.

"Run! Get away from them," Easter screeched. "They want to keep us apart." And she broke away from my brother and ran to the driver's side of the limo.

Billy hesitated a minute.

"Come on, Billy," Easter said, then she was in the car and starting it.

Billy walked away from the three of us in slow motion. He kept turning back to look, like maybe we had moved away or something, between steps. At last he was to the car.

Easter beeped the horn.

"We can talk about it, son," Daddy said.

A big, fat lump came up in my throat.

Billy bent down and stared through the window at Easter. He looked back at us.

"Stay," Momma said, and she lifted her hands to him.

Willie-Bill climbed into the car and closed the door shut.

Easter slammed on the gas and rocks and dirt and shell sprayed into the air.

"Billy," I called, but I don't think he even heard me.

His face peered out at us, faded and dark, through the window. And, for some reason, I couldn't even raise my hand to wave good-bye.

Chapter 22

THAT FIRST EVENING, AFTER BILLY AND EASTER drove away, time seemed to slow down. Momma, Daddy, and I stood out in front of the diner for almost five minutes, none of us moving or saying nothing. Or maybe it was only five seconds, because of time stretching itself out all thin and ugly.

"They'll be back," Daddy said.

I felt prickly with surprise. I glanced at Momma. "Do you think they'll be back, Momma?" I had a strong suspicion that she didn't. The thought hit me with a smack as I stood there, outside in the warm twilight, holding on to the green-handled broom like it was a dance partner. "Don't you think they've gone for a ride? You know, what Pop-Pop would call a joy ride."

"I *said* they'll be back," Daddy said. He sounded annoyed with me.

Momma turned away. "Let's finish this cleaning up," she said, and that was her answer.

Daddy opened the door for Momma and me. The bell clanged. We all went back to work.

BILLY DIDN'T COME HOME that night. Or the next. I know 'cause I kept a steady eye watching the road as best I could. And he never called either.

Every time Christmas and I went and did anything together, I kept one of my eyeballs glued to watching the road. I felt so sad about this whole thing I couldn't even talk to Christmas about it.

Especially because she was so casual and all. "They've probably gone off to get married," she said. "Easter's been wanting to get out of here forever. She wouldn't mind taking your brother with her."

"But Billy's only fourteen," I said.

And Christmas looked at me like, So?

Late that night there was a knock at our front door. I felt my heart bang up against my ribs.

"Billy," I said, soft under my breath. I stood up from where I sat next to Pop-Pop in the front room. He'd come over from Orlando to stay with Momma 'cause she said she felt sick inside.

"I keep feeling something awful has happened," she'd say to me when I'd stop close to her.

The fear of God would run through me, making my heart pound in my throat.

Maybe that was Billy, now, at the door. I could surprise Momma a good one by dragging my brother back to her, where she sat in the sunroom with Daddy.

I ran to the door and slung it wide.

Miriam Season stood on the front porch, dressed in a slinky, short black dress.

"May I come in?" Miriam Season asked, and without waiting for an answer, walked right on in past me. Her small, pointed heels clicked on the hardwood floor. Momma was gonna be surprised after all.

"Oh yes, please," I said to her back.

Miriam Season didn't wait for me to show her to my family. She just walked through the main floor of the house, looking for Momma and Daddy.

"Hey," I kept saying, but she brushed me away with her hand.

"Momma," I screeched when Miriam was in the kitchen. She was headed for the stairs that led to the second floor. Somehow she had missed the sunroom.

"Momma," I called again. "We got company." Then to Miriam Season I said, "You don't need to look through the upstairs. She's down here."

"Your momma doesn't seem to be anywhere." When Miriam said "momma" it almost sounded like a curse word.

"Honey," Momma called.

"We're in the kitchen. *Miriam Season* and I are in the kitchen."

I heard my mother running toward us, her bare feet slapping at the floor. She appeared in the doorway, her hair looking almost wild. "Have you heard from them?"

"I thought I might have to take a tour of your upstairs when I couldn't find you down here." Miriam gestured at the room and her bracelet sparkled.

"May I help you?" Momma asked, her voice turned cold.

"Always the waitress," Miriam said. "I guess old habits are hard to break."

"May I help you?" Momma asked again. "Or just show you to the door?"

"I've come for my daughter," Miriam said, angry.

Momma's face went a little soft. "She's not here."

Daddy came up behind her.

"Let's all go sit in the front room," he said, and pulling at Momma's arm, he led the way.

We all moved into the living room, Pop-Pop and me, too.

Miriam settled herself down on the cream-colored sofa.

Momma sat down on a matching chair, but she didn't make herself comfortable. Instead, she moved her bottom out to the very edge of the seat.

The walls in nearly every room of our house are covered with pictures of my family. The living room was no different. Both Daddy and Momma play with photography, so we don't have any store-bought pictures at all.

"I've come to pick up my daughter," Miriam said, after checking out the photos.

"Your daughter isn't here," Momma said.

"I want to talk to your son, then," Miriam said.

Daddy, on the arm of Momma's chair, looked down at his hands. "He left with your daughter," he said. With his head down like that, it almost seemed he was apologizing.

"I could sue you," Miriam said, her voice tight. "You let the two of them run off together."

Daddy raised his eyebrows just a bit. I guess Miriam Season didn't know Daddy used to be a lawyer.

"We didn't let 'em go," I said.

Daddy shushed me with a, "Sit quiet, Honey."

Miriam Season looked at me with an I-don't-have-time-for-you stare.

Pop-Pop moved a bit where he stood in the corner. Momma stood up. Then Miriam Season stood. With her heels on, Miriam Season was right about the height of Momma, but so much skinnier she looked sick.

"Your daughter drove away with my son," Momma said, her voice low. If Miriam knew anything from all her acting, you'd think she'd get the hint right then and there she was in dangerous territory.

"What are you saying?" Miriam asked. Her voice was tough sounding, too. I started to wonder if Momma would be any match for her. I mean, Miriam Season has been an actress for as long as I can remember, arguing with all the greats of Hollywood. Momma's only had me and Billy and Daddy to practice with.

"I am saying," Momma said, talking real slow. She could have spelled the words faster. "That your daughter drove over here in a black limousine and picked our son up."

The room went real quiet, then Daddy said, "I've already driven around looking for them, checking out the highway partway to Orlando and to the beach. I expect Bill will be calling, or coming home eventually." Daddy touched Momma on the arm and she sat back down again. Miriam Season did too, only this time she didn't nestle herself into the cushions.

Pop-Pop spoke. "Every night, Ms. Season, we pray for their safety. If you'd like to join in the circle this evening we'd be more than pleased."

Miriam Season stood up so fast I thought she might bust right through the ceiling. Once to her feet she teetered on the slender, tall heels of her shiny black shoes. "Pray?" she said, and her voice almost popped both my eardrums. She was to the door before any one of us had a chance to get out of our seats. In the doorway she turned around.

"The whole free world to choose from," Miriam Season said, "and I had to pick the dot on the map that's full of lunatics. I'm not interested in praying to find my daughter. I'm interested in getting in the car and driving that girl back from wherever she is, back to where she belongs."

Miriam Season moved into the living room again. The large, flowered carpet that covered nearly all the floor but the edges muffled the click of her heels.

"And if anything has happened to my little girl," she said. "If any complications arise from this—" Miriam Season waved her hand around the room like she was batting at cigarette smoke. "—fling, I will make sure the four of you are held responsible."

For a minute I thought Momma was gonna jump on Miriam Season and knock her high-fashioned body straight through the wall. But Momma didn't. She just sped to the screen door, which she pushed open. "Do you need any help leaving?" Momma asked. I could see she was angry by the way her one hand shook.

"Ms. Season," Daddy said, walking to the door, passing close to our neighbor. "Considering the age differences in our children, if there are any complications from tonight, and knowing the law as I do, I think perhaps you better have yourself one damn good lawyer."

"I said," Momma said, still standing with the door open, "do you need any help leaving?"

"You're letting in mosquitoes," I said.

Miriam Season walked out. But before she left she turned to me and said, "I'll not have any more of this fanatical influence penetrating the walls of my home. You'll not be seeing Christmas again." The way she said it made it sound like I had a terminal illness.

Later, after prayer circle and while Momma was making the spare room bed with fresh sheets for Pop-Pop, after Daddy had called the police to let them know about Easter and Billy and talked to a few of his lawyer friends in Orlando, I checked out the floor in the hall. I thought maybe, the way Miriam Season had stomped out, she'd left her mark on the wooden floor. But there wasn't anything to tell that she'd even been in the house, except the feeling.

Chapter 23

THAT NIGHT, WHILE I DREAMED OF CHRISTMAS and me on a fat cow shaped something like a limousine, Daddy came into my bedroom and woke me up.

"Honey," he said, shaking my shoulder with his gentle hand. "Honey."

"The cow isn't safe," I said.

Daddy shook me again. "Honey."

For a moment I thought I was outside, under the stars, then I saw the outline of Daddy sitting on my bed. The door was half open and light fell through the crack and puddled on the floor.

I blinked hard, but my eyes didn't want to stay awake. "What?" I said. I let my eyelids close. They had won the battle against staying open.

I felt Daddy's breath on my face. It was warm and smelled of onions and garlic.

"Move, Daddy. You're polluting my breathing air." I rolled on my side.

"Honey, turn over and sit up. I have something to tell you." Daddy's voice was strange sounding, thick and heavy, like he'd been crying. It woke me like a splash of cool drinking water and I sat right up, bumping into him.

"What?" I asked.

"They found them. The police found them. There's been an accident."

"What?"

"The police . . ."

"I heard you," I said, and my voice was screaming. "I heard you."

"Shh, shh, shh," Daddy said. He wrapped his arms around me and then he was crying on my shoulder.

Have you ever had someone say something to you, and when the words came out, it felt like they had tipped you back and filled you to the top with ice cubes? That's what it felt to me right then. Somehow I knew something awful had happened.

"Let's go," Momma said, leaning into my bedroom. She wasn't crying at all, just as calm as she could be.

"Where?" I said, throwing back the covers. Everything looked so gray in my room. Blood pounded in my ears.

"They've life-flighted Billy and Easter on over to Orlando Heights Memorial," Daddy said.

I started to swing out of bed, but Momma's voice cut right over to me. "Honey, you're staying here with Pop-Pop."

"No, I'm not," I said. "I'm going to see my brother." I wrestled to get out of my sheet.

"There's no need. Children under twelve won't be allowed into intensive care."

"I am twelve," I said. The covers seemed to be hanging on to my feet on purpose.

Momma came into the room fast and threw her arms around me. "Pop-Pop's here and I want you to stay," she said. "There's no telling what we'll see. Your brother wrecked the very day they left and he and Easter were trapped in that car for nearly two days before someone found them."

"But, Daddy," I said, "I thought you went looking for them."

In the dim light of the room I saw Daddy lower his head. His tears started to flow again.

"Somehow the area where the car went over closed up around it," Momma said. She stood up. "But we don't have time to talk. We've got to go." Her voice was business-like, too formal. The sound of it set me to shivering.

Daddy stood and walked from the room. As he passed her, Momma reached out for him, her fingers touching his arm. Turning, they started down the hall and Momma's voice floated back to me. "Even the police had a hard time finding the car, Joe." And then the mumble of Daddy's low voice came whisping in, but I couldn't quite understand it all, like maybe things had gone foreign on me during the night.

The foreign stuff, I realized, lying back into my bed,

had all begun when Miriam Season came into our house. No, it had started way before that. Maybe when she had walked into the diner, thin and fancy and loud, for one and all to see.

After Momma and Daddy left, I lay in bed thinking and worrying and crying till Pop-Pop came up to check on me.

"How bad is he?" I asked my grandfather, who sat in a chair in a dark corner of my room. Outside the window I could just see the night sky, midnight blue, like one of my crayons.

"Not too good, Honey. Not too good."

"What is it?" I had to know and still I was afraid to know.

"Broken bones, some internal damage, all that time in the heat. Luckily a couple of windows broke out in the crash. They didn't go into detail because it was over the phone. Hospitals are picky that way."

"And what about Easter? How's she?" Anger bubbled up inside me at Christmas's sister.

"They wouldn't tell your momma anything about her."

"It's all Easter's fault," I said. "She's never wanted to be here. Never wanted to live with Miriam Season or Christmas."

"That whole family needs our prayers," Pop-Pop said.

"Prayers," I shouted. "Prayers. Does God even listen?

Does He even care? He could have stopped this whole thing, but He didn't." I flung my hands out in the darkness, showing I meant it all.

"Now, Honey," Pop-Pop said, his voice smooth. "God doesn't often interfere. He lets us make choices. And with choices there are consequences."

"He could have stopped them," I said.

"They chose to go together. Easter took that limo—"

"I hate Easter," I said. "And I hate Miriam Season."

Pop-Pop was silent again. "You probably won't understand this, Honey," he said. "But because of Miriam you have Christmas."

I sat up in bed, my legs crossed. I had a headache and my nose was stuffed and I felt too hot.

"One thing I think we owe to mommas is the fact they gave us life, even if there's nothin' else to say thank you for."

I knew what he meant, but I didn't care. "I still hate her. I hate the way she treats Christmas. I hate it that Miriam thinks she's the all-important boss when all she really cares about is her own self."

I started crying again. "And she won't let her visit anymore. And this is partly my fault. I knew all along that Billy and Easter were seeing each other, Pop-Pop, and I didn't tell. I'm as guilty as they are."

"*They* made their decisions."

"And you know Christmas was more our family than she was Miriam's. And now lookit what happened to Billy."

Pop-Pop came over to where I sat crumpled up, leaning on my pillow and crying. The hall light still lit my room.

"It's all right, Honey," Pop-Pop said.

"No it isn't," I said.

"They found him."

"But he's bad off."

Pop-Pop wrapped his arms around me and we sat there like that for a long time.

THAT AFTERNOON I WAITED out at the diner. I waited for Momma to call so Pop-Pop could come tell me what was going on, waited for my heart to stop hammering and waited for Christmas to come visit. Even if all we did was work on her ol' tree house, and never said a word about what was going on, it would be better.

Momma finally did telephone, a brief call to say that they'd not be home for the weekend, and that I should leave the closed sign in the window of the diner. She told Pop-Pop to tell me that things weren't looking so good for either Billy or Easter. Then she went to sit with Daddy next to my brother.

And on Friday, right before the rain began to fall for our three o'clock shower, Christmas showed up at my house.

"Honey," she called, from my driveway. "Honey, come on out."

I was eating lunch, still feeling foreign. Not opening the diner hadn't helped any. Christmas being gone hadn't helped either. I ran to where she stood with her bike. The sky was graying up quick.

"Christmas," I said when I came out. Already, down the road I could see the traffic starting thick for the week-end. I wanted to hug her up close.

"Let's go walking, Honey," she said.

I almost said, the traffic's too bad for us to do any walking, but instead I jumped on down the steps beside her.

"Hey," I said.

"Hello." Christmas's face was funny looking. Pinched almost.

I had missed her so bad that seeing her stand there made my heart feel good, even with all the trouble. I hugged Christmas tight and she squeezed me back.

"I thought you weren't allowed over," I said, smiling so hard it hurt.

"I'm not," Christmas said, but she didn't smile. "Miriam's at the hospital now. Or somewhere. She doesn't know I'm here."

"Pop-Pop," I called, not wanting to waste any time in case Miriam came driving up. "I'm going for a walk."

He came to the front porch. "Don't be long, girls," he said. "It's gonna rain."

We started off, up my long driveway, left at the high-way jammed with traffic.

We stayed at the edge of the road, stepping off into the grasses when cars zoomed past.

We walked single file, Christmas in front of me.

A few drops of rain fell, soft for only a second.

"Can we cross through the cows' field?" Without waiting for an answer Christmas went through a ditch toward the fenced pasture.

I checked for bulls. I couldn't see anything. "I don't know why not," I said. "But it would be easier—"

"I don't want easier."

Then the rain poured. Heavy, hard drops that I wanted to take cover from. I followed Christmas to the fence, my hair stringing up before my eyes, and the road running silver away from me, smelling of steam and dirt, and the sky going almost night colored.

"Christmas," I said to her back, which was nearly soaked now. "Christmas."

She turned then and I could see tears mixing in with rain. "Easter's dead," she said. "She died this morning."

"What?" I screamed. "What?" And it seemed to me that heaven poured out all the rain it could right at that moment.

"She's dead," Christmas said, and she turned and walked on while I wondered for words.

"Let's go back your way. Let's just go the way you know." Christmas, crying, went back through the ditch, and up onto the road. I wanted to walk beside her, to hold her hand, to hug her hard, but traffic barreled past.

Rain grayed things up between me and Christmas. I followed in her footsteps. A four wheeler, set up high on its tires, drove though a puddle, splashing us. I felt grit hit my face.

Christmas stumbled and fell to her knees. Rain splashed all around. I dropped to the ground, close enough that I could feel the heat from her body. I touched her arm.

All of a sudden Christmas began to wail. She covered her face with her hands, and for a second I thought she was going to throw herself flat.

"Easter," Christmas said, like she was calling for her sister. "Oh, Easter." She turned to me. "Did she suffer all that time before they found her in the car? That's what I wonder, did she suffer?"

"I don't know," I said. "I hope not. I hope to Jesus not."

"It was so hot in there."

I was quiet.

"It was so hot and even the rain couldn't make her cool."

"I'm sorry."

"Your brother is alive. And my sister isn't. They were in the same wreck. But one of them survived and the other didn't."

I couldn't say anything. There was nothing to say.

The rain started to let up some, until it was only a light sprinkle coming down on us.

"I wanted her gone," Christmas said. "Honey, I wanted her to never come back. I could see the way she was going and I knew we'd never be able to stay here. We'd move again and again and again. And I wouldn't be able to see you anymore. And I'd never be with Pop-

Pop. I couldn't stand those thoughts, so I wished her gone. I didn't even care if she'd die, I thought, if she'd leave me in peace. I was glad when the two of them left."

The sun parted the clouds then, throwing down streams of bright, hot light on the two of us. And right at that very moment I saw everything so clearly. I saw the heat coming up off the road, and the blueness of the sky. I saw the hurt of having lost a sister and the guilt of it all and the relief of having not lost a brother. It all piled up thick and sat heavy as the air around us. A few drops of rain splashed down, big ol' fat drops that when they hit the dirt flattened out round as a coin.

I started to cry, too.

There was a second wind to the storm right then. The sun hid itself behind another cloud and the rain came down, just a light sprinkle, washing over me and Christmas, washing over us like it was trying to smooth the hurt away, like it was trying to clear away anything that either of us had ever done wrong. Like it was making us clean.

Chapter
24

I DIDN'T SEE CHRISTMAS AGAIN AFTER THAT rain. She didn't come back the next day or the next, and no one answered the door when I dropped by to see her. One afternoon I saw four American Van Line trucks headed to her place, and I followed them quick on my bike to find The Mansion full of men packing things up. None of them was Bob, Ted, Carol, or Alice from what seemed a million years ago when Christmas and her family came to Heaven. There was a For Sale sign stuck in the wild grasses of the big lawn.

I worried a lot about Billy and whether he'd get better. And I did a lot of thinking.

Pop-Pop had had all the answers for Christmas. I decided to ask him for a few for myself.

It was during lunch with my grandfather that I cornered him.

"I need to know the truth about getting saved," I said, straight out over bacon, lettuce, and tomato sandwiches.

He looked me in the eye. "What do you need to know?"

"Does it work sure?" I asked.

"If it changes your life and you follow Jesus' way, it does."

"And what if I never find God like that? What if what happened to Christmas never happens to me? Or worse yet, what if I die, not saved, like Easter?" That was my real fear, one that turned me cold inside.

Pop-Pop pushed back his chair and it squeaked on the wooden floor. "Honey," he said. "I have a confession to make. My own conversion was a one-on-one experience between God and me. I didn't join to Him in front of a crowd of people. It was very private."

"You're kidding," I said, so surprised that the hairs on my head seemed to stand tall. "Then why do you have people come forward?"

"People find God in their own ways," Pop-Pop said, after a moment of reflecting. "This is a way for some, but not everybody. Honey, I've told you before that I know I don't have all the truth to preach to people. I'm always looking for it, searching for it. And when I find it, I'm gonna pass it on. Remember that. Your old grandfather doesn't have all the answers. And I've never professed to having them." He took in a deep breath and smiled at me, the very smile he had used on Christmas, the very smile he used on everyone. It was full of love and concern and genuine compassion. And it set my heart at ease.

FOR DAYS I WANDERED around wondering why Christmas had never said good-bye. I sat out in my front yard for hours, hoping maybe, somehow, Christmas might come Rollerblading up. But she didn't. I felt different, sitting there in the heat, with the bees buzzing around and the flies pestering me. In my guts I felt old, like all this stuff that had happened had made me age when I didn't want to.

Momma and Daddy stayed at the hospital so that Billy was never alone. Pop-Pop asked all his viewers and congregation members to pray for his only grandson, and sure enough Billy started getting better.

I went up to the hospital to visit him every other day after he got out of the ICU. The rest of my time I spent doing nothing.

There was a great big ache in my heart. Christmas was gone. I couldn't hardly stand it.

In the mornings I'd do my chores in slow motion, trying to eat up the day that way. Afterward I'd head up to the diner and sit at one of the rod iron tables and wait. Then I'd eat a sad lunch, nothing fancy, and wait some more. I'd sit out in my tree house a bit, maybe read, then eat dinner. I went to bed early. And I tried not to think of Christmas 'cause it made my heart hurt. Never had the days gone by so slow for me.

"Honey," came a voice one morning, when I was outside the diner hoping for a little traffic. It was Taylor.

I rolled my eyes in his direction but didn't do more than grunt.

He came over, hitching up his blue jeans as he walked.

"Your brother is looking good. I'm glad he's getting better."

I nodded.

Taylor stood next to the table. "I been watching you now for days," he said, his voice soft. "You're breaking my heart, girl."

I looked up at him and my eyes filled with tears.

"Christmas was a good friend for you, I know that." Taylor sat hisself down without an invitation. But I didn't mind so much.

"I see you're lonely for her, missing her bad." He folded his hands on the table in front of me. I could see a faint grease line under his fingernails. "I know what it's like to miss someone."

I nodded my head a little. I thought of Taylor's momma leaving so long ago. There was a lump in my throat.

"You know what I do, when I'm real sad?"

I wanted to say move tires from place to place, but I couldn't trust my voice, so I didn't say anything.

"I write." Taylor leaned toward me and his blue eyes seemed bluer than normal. "I got me a whole collection of poems and stories in my house, tucked away in my room. Daddy don't even know. I've even got me the beginnings of a novel going on. It's an adventure, but I bet you'd like it."

"Yeah?" I said, testing my voice.

"Sure do. Maybe you should try it. The writing thing,

I mean. Maybe you should write in a diary or something."

Taylor pulled a small wire-bound notebook from his back pocket. "I brought this to you."

I took the notebook, warm from Taylor's body, and held it. "New Poems," it said on the front, but that had been scratched out. Now, in red ink were the words: "Honey's True Feelings."

"You don't have to write all your true feelings," Taylor said. "Maybe just a few of them."

"Maybe," I said. And I meant it.

"I'm just gonna sit out here with you a little longer," Taylor said.

And then me and him sat out there in the hot sun for a good long while.

The next afternoon, right in the middle of a rainstorm, I thought of the tree house out at The Mansion and how Christmas and I had never finished it. So in the middle of the rain, I got on my bike and followed the empty highway to her house.

The note was waiting for me, nailed on the side of a wall we had planned to cut a window into. The edges were curled and already the sun seemed to have lightened the ink.

Dear Honey—
Miriam says there won't be any good-byes and she caught me three times trying to sneak to your place, so finally I thought you might think to look here.

I want to thank you for being the best friend a person could ever have. You made my time in Heaven like the real heaven, I'm sure. Ask Pop-Pop, he could tell you if I'm right, ha ha.

I'll miss you, but when I am grown up, I plan to come back to Heaven and maybe buy this place so we can be neighbors again. When I do, let's finish this tree house first thing. Promise?

Love,

Christmas, your best friend in Jesus and living and rainstorms

I looked at the note nailed to the wall for a long time. I decided to leave it there, where Christmas had hammered it, 'cause it seemed fitting. It was what she would have wanted me to do, I think.

I found a scrap of pencil we'd drawn plans with and at the bottom of her note wrote one of my own.

"Christmas, I'll look for you in Heaven."

Then I went off to the sign Momma had done up so long ago, and with a can of red spray paint changed it to say: You're Entering and Leaving Heaven—Right This Very Second (pop 7). You know, for when Christmas does come back.